there,

...st wanted to say hello and tell y...

I live on the very outside of London near the River Thames, ...n my husband (who is Dutch and makes great pancakes!) ...our two young daughters. We also have a Siamese cat called ...mish who came to us as a very timid rescue cat and spent ...first few weeks hiding up the chimney! Now he is a real ...ily cat and loves sitting on my lap (and trying to sit on my ...board!) when I'm at my desk writing.

I'm half Welsh and half English but I grew up in Scotland. ...fore I became a writer I worked as a doctor, mainly with ...dren and teenagers. From as far back as I can remember ...always loved stories in any form – reading books, watching fi...s, playing make-believe games. As a child I always had ...antasy world or another on the go and as I grew older ...changed to actual ongoing sagas that I wrote down in ...cise books and worked on for weeks at a time.

I really hope you enjoy reading this – and that you'll write me at **Gwyneth.Rees@bloomsbury.com** to let me know what you think. I'd love it if you told me a bit about yourself too!

Best wishes,

Gwyneth x

Books by Gwyneth Rees

Cherry Blossom Dreams

For younger readers:
The *Fairy Dust* series
Cosmo and the Magic Sneeze
The Magic Princess Dress
My Super Sister
My Super Sister and the Birthday Party

THE
HONEY
MOON
SISTERS

Gwyneth
Rees x

BLOOMSBURY

LONDON OXFORD NEW YORK NEW DELHI SYDNEY

Bloomsbury Publishing, London, Oxford, New York, New Delhi and Sydney

First published in Great Britain in March 2016 by Bloomsbury Publishing Plc
50 Bedford Square, London WC1B 3DP

www.bloomsbury.com

BLOOMSBURY is a registered trademark of Bloomsbury Publishing Plc

A CIP catalogue record for this book is available from the British Library

ISBN 978 1 4088 5275 0

Typeset by RefineCatch Limited, Bungay, Suffolk
Printed and bound in Great Britain by CPI Group (UK) Ltd, Croydon CR0 4YY

1 3 5 7 9 10 8 6 4 2

For Eliza and Lottie, with love

Chapter One

'Nice work, Poppy,' our English teacher, Mr Anderson, told me as he handed me back my book report. 'I especially like the way you discussed the villain – very thoughtful and insightful. Well done.'

'Thanks,' I muttered, feeling myself blush as I pushed my glasses further back on my nose. Mr Anderson has got to be the coolest – and cutest – teacher in our school, and I know I'm not the only one in my class to have a bit of a crush on him.

My friend Anne-Marie, who sits beside me, gave me a nudge with her elbow. I knew she was going to start teasing me about Mr Anderson as soon as the bell rang.

It was last thing on Friday afternoon and Mr Anderson had given us ten minutes to complete the task of making a sketch and giving it a title. We then had to pass our drawing to the person next to us, who would have to take

1

it home and write a poem to go with it to read out in class the following Friday. Mr Anderson is always coming up with stuff like that to do at the end of the day on a Friday afternoon. Normally I'd have been sketching away furiously along with everyone else, trying to make Anne-Marie's homework task as tricky as possible, but today my heart wasn't really in it. I couldn't stop thinking about my foster-sister Amy and how much I was going to miss her. Then, with just a few minutes to go, I suddenly thought of something to draw.

'Wow, Sadie!' Mr Anderson was exclaiming as he reached the desk behind mine.

I twisted round to see what he was wowing about and saw that Sadie Shaw (who sits right behind me, unfortunately) had drawn a stuffed bird just like the one in our art department. It was beautifully drawn but she had used red pen to add an angry gash dripping with blood right across the bird's neck. The title she had written was 'MURDER'.

'What are *you* looking at?' she hissed when she saw me staring.

Sadie is new to our school, having started a few weeks ago, halfway through Year Eight. Despite the fact that we're related, I have no memory of meeting Sadie before her first day at our school. I wouldn't even have known who she was if Mum hadn't recognised her name when I told her there was a new girl. So far Sadie had mostly avoided talking to me and had made it perfectly clear that the last thing she wanted was to be my friend. I'd stopped trying to be nice to her after the second week, when she'd grabbed me in the girls' toilets and threatened to make my life miserable if I told anyone the truth about us. I'd told her I didn't want anyone to know either, so keeping it a secret suited me fine.

Sadie acted cold and aloof towards everybody and pretty soon all sorts of rumours were flying around the school about her. The most popular one was that she was the delinquent niece of our headmaster, Mr Jamieson, and had been expelled from her last school. This was because she looks a bit like him (they both have reddish hair and blue eyes and scowl a lot), plus she'd been seen going into his office a few times. There was also the more colourful rumour someone had started that her dad was a hitman! I'd gone straight home and asked Mum if that could be true and she'd said she doubted it, but since she hadn't had any contact with Sadie's dad in years she couldn't tell me anything for certain.

Of course I know better than to believe rumours, but

Sadie certainly seemed a lot tougher than most of the kids in our school and nobody wanted to get on the wrong side of her. She'd recently moved to our fairly small grammar school from a big comprehensive school on the other side of town. Anne-Marie, who always seems to know everything about everybody, said she'd moved to one of the new houses on the other side of the park. (Mum was more interested in that fact than anything else, saying that she wondered where Sadie's dad had got the money.)

Sadie might seem cold and detached on the surface but there were definitely a few things she was passionate about. The most obvious one was art. Ever since she'd arrived she'd been regularly impressing our art teacher with the work she produced, although the other day when Miss Hodge had brought out the stuffed birds for us to sketch, Sadie had left her paper totally blank, saying it was cruel to kill animals just to stuff them.

'Maybe they died of natural causes and then they got stuffed,' Anne-Marie had said with a grin.

'It doesn't even matter how they died!' Sadie had blurted out angrily. 'We don't stuff humans and put *them* on display, do we? So why should we do it to animals?'

'Same reason we eat animals and not humans, I

suppose,' Katy Clarkson put in smugly. 'Cos they aren't so high up the food chain.'

It had started off a heated debate in our class and Miss Hodge had looked really relieved when the bell rang.

Mr Anderson perched himself on the edge of Sadie's desk, enthusing over her drawing and asking her questions about it. To say that the rest of the girls in our class were jealous would be an understatement. (If there is one teacher in our school who you would want perched on your desk it is definitely Mr Anderson.)

'Sadie's clearly making a point here,' Mr Anderson said as he held up her drawing to show to the rest of us.

'Too right!' Sadie agreed with him angrily. 'Taxidermy is completely gross and the school shouldn't allow stuffed birds – or animals – on the premises!'

'O ... K ...' Mr Anderson gave Katy and her friend Julia Munro a stern look to stop them giggling. 'So, Sadie, I can see you feel very strongly about this issue. Perhaps you can get the school council to bring it up for further discussion.'

'School council's useless,' Sadie scoffed. 'We had one at my last school. Goody-goody teacher's pets, all of them.'

Mr Anderson said something in reply but I didn't really take it in because I was too busy feeling mortified and sliding down in my chair. I had been elected as the Year Eight representative on our school council at the start of the year after writing an admittedly cringe-inducing statement about why I thought I'd be good at the job. Hopefully nobody would mention that right now.

Of course straight away Anne-Marie (who has a bit of a big mouth) announced, 'Poppy's on the school council.'

'Shut up, Anne-Marie,' I hissed, ducking my head forward and letting my hair fall over my face so nobody would see me blushing. (I have shoulder-length brown hair, which I usually tie back, but today I had a couple of spots on my face that I was trying to hide.)

'Don't tell me that's your school councillor's badge, Poppy.' Sadie was pointing to the little felt flower brooch pinned to the lapel of my blazer, which was over the back of my seat. 'Looks like it was made by a five-year-old.'

'A four-year-old, actually,' I replied fiercely. Amy had made the brooch as a goodbye gift and presented it to me that morning just as I'd been going out the door to school.

The bell rang and there was a massive kerfuffle and loads of laughter as people swapped their drawings and got ready to go.

'You three swap with each other,' Mr Anderson said, since Sadie didn't have a desk partner. Sadie quickly gave hers to Anne-Marie and I didn't even get a look at Anne-Marie's sketch as she shoved it straight into my bag. That just left mine, which I was obviously meant to give to Sadie.

I had sketched the face of a little girl with a wild Afro and called it 'Amy'. Now I felt reluctant to part with it. I had visions of Sadie crumpling it up in a ball and trampling on it.

Sadie looked like she couldn't care less either way, but unfortunately Mr Anderson noticed.

'Is something wrong, Poppy?'

I suddenly felt teary as I remembered Amy wouldn't be there to greet me when I got home.

I *so* had to pull myself together.

'No,' I mumbled as I handed Sadie the drawing and pulled a tissue out of my bag. I removed my glasses, which I only need for reading the board in any case, and quickly wiped my eyes.

That's when I noticed Sadie staring at me. 'What?' I demanded crossly.

'Nothing,' she said with a small smile. 'It's just … you don't look nearly as clever without your glasses.'

'Gee … thanks,' I grunted.

'I'm just making an observation, that's all. Glasses really *do* make people look brainier. It's pretty weird considering that they just mean you've got defective eyesight, right?'

I glared at her. I hate my glasses, but I made a point of putting them back on my nose rather than away in my bag like I usually do at the end of a lesson. I didn't want her to think I cared what *she* thought.

'Are you coming, Poppy?' Anne-Marie asked impatiently. I'd almost forgotten she was still there.

I hurried to catch her up. Anne-Marie can be a bit of a pain sometimes but we were at primary school together and we've been friends for a really long time. We were never *best* friends, but when we transferred to the grammar school our other friends mostly went to different schools, so we'd ended up becoming closer.

I'd quickly made a new best friend called Olivia in Year Seven, and Anne-Marie had been jealous, which was awkward, but then Olivia had moved away just before we started Year Eight. Anne-Marie had said I could have another chance to be her best friend if I wanted, even though she had other friends now, and I have to say it made me see that loyalty in a friendship is important too – it's not just about how 'close' or 'in tune' the two of you are.

I miss Olivia though. Anne-Marie and I don't always see things the same way and I have to be a lot more careful what I say to her. Plus she really embarrassed me one time in Year Seven by broadcasting something I'd told her in confidence.

She had asked me and some of the other girls to vote on who was the cutest male teacher in our school, getting us to fill out a silly questionnaire in which we had to give marks out of five for each attribute she'd named. One was 'Cuteness of bum' and she wanted to know why I hadn't given Mr Anderson 5/5. So I had truthfully said that I'd knocked off a mark because when he'd taken off his jacket the day before I'd noticed that, compared to some of the other candidates, he had quite a chunky bum. And that if I was giving 5/5 to the compact muscly bottom of Mr Christie, our PE teacher, then I couldn't in all fairness give the same mark to our English teacher.

Anne-Marie had thought that was hilarious and repeated it to loads of other people. Then Julia Munro – who can be really bitchy – related the story to Mr Anderson in front of the whole class a few days later. I thought I was going to die of embarrassment that day, and even now just thinking about it makes me blush. Olivia hadn't wanted me to be friends at all with Anne-Marie after that, but Anne-Marie was so persistent in trying to win me back that I'd eventually agreed to forgive her. And I suppose I was glad I had when Olivia told me her dad had got a new job and they were moving away in the summer holiday.

'What's wrong, Poppy?' Anne-Marie asked me now as we walked out of the classroom with Sadie hot on our heels. 'You've been looking miserable all day.'

'It's nothing,' I lied, not wanting to mention Amy while Sadie was listening in.

'It's probably something sappy like her pet hamster died,' Julia said as she came up behind us.

Anne-Marie whirled round instantly. 'That's not funny!' she snarled. '*My* hamster died last week and I was really upset!' Anne-Marie is a real animal lover and for as long as I've known her she's always kept loads of pets.

'Katy told me you had a funeral in your back garden and that you even made a little gravestone for him,' Julia said scornfully. 'What does it say? *Here lies Hammy.*' She started to laugh.

'His name was Squeaky and he was like one of the family. And it's perfectly normal to have a funeral for a pet! Isn't it, Poppy?' Anne-Marie looked at me for support.

But before I could speak Sadie said a little piously, 'It's normal for *humans* to have funerals. Having one for a hamster is unnatural and pretty silly if you ask me.'

'Yeah – well, I didn't ask you!' Anne-Marie snapped.

'Maybe you should've got it stuffed instead, Anne-Marie,' I suggested coolly.

Anne-Marie had to rush off at that point so as not to be late for the piano lesson she has after school on a Friday. That left me alone with Sadie.

'So who's Amy?' she asked before I could get away from her.

I sighed. Maybe I should give her a chance. Maybe if I told her, I'd discover that she *did* have a heart underneath all those tough layers.

'Amy's the little girl my mum's been fostering,' I explained. 'She left this morning. She's being adopted.'

'Oh ...' She looked quite thoughtful and just for a second I thought she might be going to say something sympathetic.

But of course I was wrong.

'My dad told me that your mum takes in other people's kids.' She paused. 'So why's that, then? Isn't she happy with the one she's got?' And she gave me a mischievous grin before flouncing off.

Chapter Two

As I walked out of school a good twenty minutes later I was still thinking about Sadie. It's just really hard to believe sometimes that we're cousins.

Sadie is absolutely *nothing* like me – not in appearance, not in personality, and certainly not in the way she behaves. I mean, here I am with my mid-brown unruly hair which never sits nicely, my increasingly spotty face and my alarmingly growing boobs. (I've had to start wearing a bra recently.) Plus I'm always blushing these days and I seem to get embarrassed a lot more easily than I did when I first started secondary school eighteen months ago.

Sadie, on the other hand, always looks perfect. She's got sleek reddish hair cut in a swingy bob, striking blue eyes and of course she's got perfect vision too. She never has a single spot and there isn't an ounce of fat on her.

And she hasn't got embarrassingly noticeable boobs yet either. I don't think I've ever seen her blush and she's always super quick to say something smart to put other people down. It's not even like she needs to most of the time, because in most subjects she easily holds her own despite having gone to a pretty rubbish school (according to her) before joining ours. As for art – well, there she makes everyone else's work look like nursery school stuff.

'Hey, Poppy!' yelled a familiar voice.

I turned to see Josh coming out of school behind me. Josh and I have known each other since we were babies and now Olivia's left I definitely consider him to be my best friend, even though I know I'm probably not his. Mind you, he never tries to hide the fact that we're friendly. His mum and mine met at some baby and toddler class, where they became really good friends, and since he was an only child like me, we played together a lot when we were little.

I was thirteen last month and Josh is actually only six months older than me, though he's in the year above me at school. Mum often comments on Josh's looks – his big brown eyes and cute freckles in particular – and I know there are plenty of girls in our year and his own who fancy him something rotten. Occasionally I get to hang out with him and his Year Nine mates, which makes Anne-Marie really jealous.

'So … what are *you* still doing here?' Josh asked me.

'Oh, just had some stuff to do,' I muttered, not wanting to say I'd been wasting time in the toilets to avoid leaving the building at the same time as Sadie. 'What about you?'

'Had to go and get my phone back from Mrs Smee. She caught me and Sean texting each other in class again.' Sean has been his best mate since the start of this year. I don't really know Sean that well, but because he and his twin sister, Sasha, are Mr Anderson's step-kids I suppose I've taken a bit more of an interest in him than any of Josh's other mates. It was about this time last year when the news spread about Sean's mum dating our English teacher, and then they got married in the summer holiday. It was a pretty major gossip-fest for a while.

'Mrs Smee's really got it in for you two, hasn't she?' I said with a grin.

Josh pointed at my brooch. 'Amy make you that?'

'Yes. She was *so* sweet to me this morning.' I tried not to get too emotional as I remembered how she'd hugged me, her strong little arms firmly clamped around my neck. Amy had been really skinny and delicate when she'd first come to us – not the solid little thing she was now.

14

'My mum says she might not have been able to settle in to any other family if you guys hadn't helped her so much,' Josh said.

'I know. And I'm happy for her. It's just ... it was really hard saying goodbye.'

'But you'll see her again, right?'

'We're going to visit her in two weeks, but after that it depends on what her new parents decide.' Sometimes we get to keep in touch with the children we foster and sometimes we don't. It all depends on their adoptive families – or their birth families if they end up going back to them. Mum had told me she didn't want me getting my hopes up this time because Amy's adoptive parents were in two minds about it.

'Well, I'll keep my fingers crossed,' Josh said.

'Thanks.'

We walked on in silence for a bit until Josh asked, 'So are you seeing your dad this weekend?'

'Yep – *and* I'm finally getting to meet his new girl-friend.' I pulled a pained face.

'She's probably just as nervous as you are.'

'Doubt it. None of Dad's girlfriends are the nervous type.'

He grinned. 'So what type are they, then?'

'The super-confident type … plus they all have long legs and blonde hair …' I was grinning too.

'Wasn't the last one really clever with some kick-ass job?'

'You mean Penelope. She was the director of a pharmaceutical company. Mum and I called her the ice queen.'

Suddenly something caught my attention on the other side of the road. Some older teenagers were hanging out at the bus shelter, shoving each other about and laughing loudly. A couple of them were smoking. There was one younger girl in school uniform standing in the middle.

'Isn't that the new girl in your class who everyone's talking about?' Josh said as his gaze followed mine.

'Yeah … Sadie.'

Although Mum had told Josh's mum about Sadie, I'd said that I didn't want Josh to know. It wasn't that I thought he couldn't keep a secret. It was just that I didn't want to talk about Sadie at all – not with anyone. And I knew that if Josh found out he'd definitely want to talk about it because he's pretty curious that way. If he didn't know, it was easier to pretend to myself that Sadie was just any other girl in my school.

'So do you think her dad really *is* a hitman?' Josh asked, as I quickened my pace to pass them.

'Oh yeah ... right ... like she'd be at our school if he was,' I said.

'Even hitmen's kids have to get an education *somewhere*,' he said. Then he launched into a hilarious description of some gangster movie he'd seen where the main character was both a hitman *and* a struggling single dad.

Across the road we suddenly heard an angry shout and when I turned to look back I saw an older girl – she looked at least eighteen – walking rapidly down the road towards the others. She had short spiky black hair and wore jeans and a purple leather jacket. She looked furious. As soon as she reached the bus stop she grabbed Sadie by the arm and began to shake her. Then she smacked her over the head a couple of times while Sadie yelled 'Ow!' and 'Gerroff!' The other kids just watched and laughed.

Josh and I looked at each other awkwardly, wondering if we ought to try and help.

Just then a run-down old car pulled up at the bus stop and the driver (a boy who also looked at least eighteen) yelled at them to get in. The girl who'd hit Sadie let go of her abruptly and got into the front passenger seat while the others piled into the back. Sadie stood at the kerb scowling at them. I expected her to escape while she could – in any case there was no more room in the car – but instead she waited there sulkily for a few more moments before squeezing into the front of the car to share the passenger seat with the older girl. In fact, it looked like she was sitting on her lap!

'They are *so* going to get pulled over by the police,' Josh said in an incredulous voice as the car screeched away, windows down and music blaring.

I just stared after them, wondering if Sadie's dad knew what she was doing. I knew that *my* mum and dad would have two separate fits in their two separate houses if they found out *I* was hanging out with a crowd like that.

'Come on.' Josh's voice suddenly broke into my thoughts. 'Let's go home.'

I briefly wondered if Sadie would get home OK. Not that I had any special reason to care …

Chapter Three

After I'd left Josh behind at the corner of his road I started
to think some more about Sadie. She was so different to
how I'd imagined her whenever Mum had mentioned her
in the past. I mean, I don't know about you, but if I'd just
started at a new school where everyone else knew each
other except me, I'd be doing my best to fit in and make
friends. I certainly wouldn't be acting the way Sadie had
been acting ever since she'd arrived.

I've already told you about the whole anti-taxidermy
protest she started up in art. Well, it turns out she's also a
very passionate vegetarian. Actually Olivia was vegetarian
too, but the difference with Sadie is that she gets really
angry at other people for being meat eaters. Whenever
Olivia came to mine Mum always made a vegetarian
lasagne or something like that. But at school I'd eat saus-
ages and mash, or shepherd's pie, and Olivia would still sit

19

next to me while she ate the veggie option. She never *refused* to sit next to a person who had meat on their plate, and she never glared at me as if I was a *murderer* if she spotted me eating a packet of smoky bacon crisps.

The worst time was two weeks ago when Sadie caused a huge scene at lunchtime. We were in the dinner hall standing in line with our trays and Sadie was only a couple of people ahead of me in the queue. Our school dinners are generally pretty good and there's always a nice vegetarian option. Today it was macaroni cheese and I was just deciding whether to go for it or stick with the meat lasagne when there was a big commotion in the bit of the queue getting served. Sadie's voice rose above the others, asking lots of questions about the cheese sauce that was on the macaroni.

'If you can't show me some proof that it's *vegetarian* cheddar, then I'm not eating it,' Sadie said forcefully.

Katy Clarkson told her to stop holding everybody up with her stupid questions. Sadie whirled round on the spot to glare at her. 'It's *not* a stupid question, Katy! *Non*-vegetarian cheese is made using the enzymes from calves' stomachs – the enzymes that are meant to help them digest their mother's milk.'

'You're making that up!'

'No, I'm not! The poor little calves get slaughtered and the enzymes from their stomachs get put into cheese,' Sadie said.

'That's disgusting!' Katy exclaimed. 'Is that really true?'

'Google it if you don't believe me.'

Katy nodded at the tray of beef lasagne next to the macaroni cheese. It had a layer of cooked cheese on top. 'So has that got calf enzymes in it too, then?'

'Of course! It's basically a chopped-up cow topped with the contents of a little calf's stomach.'

'Yuck!' several people exclaimed at once, and suddenly Mrs Doyle, our head dinner lady, came to the hatch to see what was happening. She found she had a mutiny on her hands, as loads of people started complaining loudly about her food and refusing to eat it.

'I'm not eating that macaroni cheese until I check the packaging,' Sadie said firmly.

'Neither am I,' Katy agreed loudly, and lots of people shouted out their support.

'I'm not eating anything that's been inside a calf's stomach!' someone called out from behind me. Even further back in the queue there was a lot of chatter going on about how a calf's stomach had somehow got into today's vegetarian option.

Sadie was looking triumphant.

Mrs Doyle stood with her arms crossed in front of her and beads of sweat on her forehead. 'Well, you'll all just have to go hungry then, because I haven't got any packaging to show you.'

Miss Benkowski and Mr Christie, who were on dinner duty, came over to try and sort things out while Mrs Doyle got increasingly cross that nobody was getting fed. Another dinner lady joined her at the hatch, saying *she* couldn't be expected to know what went into the food, as her job was just to serve it – which seemed to make Mrs Doyle even crosser.

Hardly anyone chose the macaroni cheese or the lasagne that day, including me. (Thankfully I managed to get to the hatch before the baked potatoes ran out but I know a lot of people went hungry.)

A few days later we all got a letter to take home from school. It basically went on about the high quality of our school dinners and guaranteed the vegetarian-ness of the vegetarian meals, the halal-ness of the halal meals, the allergen-free-ness of the non-allergenic meals and so on and so on. (And apparently the vegetarian meals *do* contain vegetarian cheese, which Mum says most normal people would just take for granted in any case.)

Dad of course was thoroughly amused by the whole story. Unlike Mum, he never worries about offending people by questioning things. He said Sadie had every right to ask questions about the cheese, though she should have chosen a more appropriate way of doing so.

The thing about Sadie is she never worries about how whatever she does affects anyone else. If she suddenly feels the urge to do something or say something then she just does it. If she wants to complain about something in class, she'll never just have a quiet word with our teacher. She always tries to kick up as much of a stink in front of as many people as possible. And sometimes it's as if she *seeks* out ways to annoy people – especially people who never get into trouble at school, like Anne-Marie and me.

It was only about a week ago – after the school dinner incident – when Sadie very nearly got herself suspended. In our school if anyone is caught hitting anyone else they usually get suspended even if they weren't the one who started the fight.

On this particular day Anne-Marie and I had ambled out into the playground at breaktime, heading for our normal bit of wall to perch on, when we saw Sadie already there, lying along the wall with her head on her rolled-up cardigan as if she was sunbathing.

'What's she doing? She *knows* that's our spot,' Anne-Marie grumbled under her breath.

As we stopped to stare at her she must have seen us out of the corner of her eye because she suddenly swung her feet off the wall and sat up. 'What are you two gawping at?' she snapped.

'Nothing,' I said quickly. I could tell she wanted to pick a fight. 'Come on, Anne-Marie. Let's go.'

'You're a bit of a scaredy-cat, aren't you, Poppy?' Sadie said with a sly grin.

I didn't reply but I found myself feeling glad Anne-Marie was with me – right up until the second she opened her mouth, that is.

'Well, you *are* famous, you know!' Anne-Marie babbled. 'So of course other kids in school are gonna stare!'

'What are you talking about?' Sadie snarled.

'Come away, Anne-Marie!' I repeated more urgently. But she ignored me and carried on standing there like some suicidal idiot.

Sadie sprang to her feet to stand right in front of us. She seemed taller and more menacing all of a sudden. 'I said, *what do you mean?*'

'Oh, well, if the rumours are true …' Anne-Marie

mumbled in a half-teasing, half-thinking-better-of-it sort of voice.

'Rumours? What rumours?'

'About your dad! I mean, is it true –'

But before she could continue, Sadie's eyes flashed and she lunged forward as if she was about to hit Anne-Marie.

'SADIE!' a voice shouted from across the playground, and thankfully she turned for a second, giving Anne-Marie the chance to duck away.

The yell had come from our headmaster, who was now heading towards us looking grim as he waved Sadie over to speak to him.

'You shut up about my dad!' Sadie hissed at Anne-Marie. Her body was shaking and her face had turned bright red. 'And as for you …' She shot us both a look of utter hatred before turning on her heels and storming off towards Mr Jamieson.

As we waited nervously to see if we would be summoned as well, Anne-Marie whispered, 'So do you think her dad really *is* a hitman?'

'Don't be daft!'

'If he isn't, why did she freak out like that?'

I frowned. It was true that Sadie had reacted like she had *something* to hide.

Chapter Four

Anyway, here I was arriving home on Friday afternoon (after Josh and I had seen Sadie go off in that car) to find Mum unpacking shopping bags in the kitchen.

It felt weird to not have Amy hurling herself at me the second I walked through the door. Amy had been really quiet and withdrawn when she'd first come to live with us, but that had gradually changed and she'd turned into quite an energetic chatterbox by the end.

'So how did it go with Amy this morning?' I asked, carefully watching Mum's face.

'It was OK,' Mum assured me. 'No tears. They brought the puppy with them. She was so excited to see it again, bless her!'

Mum had the radio blaring out in the kitchen. The first few days after a foster-kid leaves us the house always feels way too quiet, and I know that's one of the most difficult parts for Mum.

I eyed the shopping bag nearest to me, seeing major evidence of comfort food. There were chocolate brownies, doughnuts, and was that a giant Toblerone? Mum had to be feeling bad because she was meant to be on a diet.

'Did they say if they'd decided about letting us keep in touch?' I asked.

'No, but our visit is all set up for two weeks tomorrow. They've invited us to their house for lunch.'

'Right.' I tried not to sound churlish as I asked, 'So did she really not cry *at all* when they took her?'

Mum put her arm around me. 'No, darling. But she *did* cry a little after you left for school. I had to remind her that she'd see you again in two weeks and that you'd want to hear all about what she'd been doing ...'

I swallowed over the lump in my throat. I knew it was much better for Amy to be adopted instead of staying in foster care. Plus we'd done plenty of preparation work, including meeting her new parents and sister, who were really lovely. I knew Amy had a sweet little bedroom in her new house, all decorated and waiting for her, and a big garden to play in.

The trouble was I still found it hard to imagine life in *our* house without her.

'So how was school today?' Mum asked, not fooling me for a moment with her bright voice.

'Same as usual,' I told her as I helped myself to a brownie. 'Except for science ... something went wrong with Mr Gillespie's experiment and all this green liquid bubbled up and spilt over on to the workbench. It was *so* Harry Potter!'

Mum smiled at that. 'Sounds it. Listen, your father phoned this morning. He asked if he could pick you up on his way home this evening instead of tomorrow because his car has to go to the garage tonight. I asked him to bring you back tomorrow evening instead of Sunday though. That way it's just the one night. That's OK, isn't it?'

I nodded, not liking to tell her that it no longer bothered me spending two nights at Dad's like it had when I was younger. And that I actually wouldn't have minded spending Sunday with him as well. 'Am I still meeting *her*?' I asked.

'Oh yes ... it's scheduled for tomorrow, apparently.' She pulled a sympathetic face. 'I'm sorry, darling, but you'd better go upstairs now and pack a bag.

He'll be here soon and I don't want to have to invite him in.'

I nearly rolled my eyes at that. Who was she kidding? I couldn't even remember the last time she'd invited Dad inside our house. She gets into a major flap just interacting with him on the doorstep.

Mum and Dad split up when I was six and I can't ever remember being in the same room as the two of them without there being an argument. I can still remember the tense feeling I'd get if they started to argue while we were at the table eating dinner. Sometimes I couldn't swallow my food and Mum would start fussing about it and Dad would tell her to calm down and then their arguing would get even worse.

After Dad moved out things were better. I still saw him every week, though I didn't stay the night with him for a few years. I always knew he loved me, but I've also always had the feeling that Mum loves me more. But then Mum has always been a lot more openly affectionate than Dad.

Mum began fostering two years after they split up – apparently after I started saying that I wanted a little brother or sister, though I don't remember that. Mum says that mostly what we do is provide a sort of practice family for children who've been taken into care – a chance to experience a 'normal' family life and work on any problems before they go to their new forever homes. An adoption is a second chance to have a family, Mum says, and that's way too precious to waste by not being ready for it. Of course sometimes we're just a safe place for a child to live while their own family gets themselves sorted out, which Mum says is a really nice job to have too.

Mum has always fostered preschoolers – usually girls. Most people think my mum does an amazing job, but needless to say Dad is more critical. He says he worries that I don't get enough of Mum's attention and he's asked me a few times how I feel about it. Once, when I was in a bad mood about something one of our foster-kids had done, I complained to him that Mum always took their side rather than mine. I soon wished I hadn't though, because he kicked up a huge fuss and accused Mum of putting her role as a foster-mum before the needs of her own daughter. After that I vowed I'd never complain to Dad about Mum again.

The truth is that both Mum and I enjoy having a little kid to focus on and I always get loads of praise from Mum for being such a fantastic big sister. And yes, it's sad when our foster-kids leave (though if I'm honest in one or two cases it's been a bit of a relief as well) but overall we both still feel like it's worth it.

Amy had stayed with us the longest. She'd had a lot of issues which needed to be addressed before she could be put up for adoption and she'd been pretty hard work in the beginning. But after a couple of months she had settled in to her new life with us and I was soon so attached to her that at one point I asked Mum if we could adopt her ourselves. Mum had even given it some thought and discussed it with our social worker. But in the end Mum felt we weren't the best home for Amy in the long term. Plus I know Mum loves being a foster-parent, and she said she didn't think she could do it any more if she adopted Amy.

Now, as I started to get my stuff together to take over to Dad's place, Mum's phone started ringing.

'Oh, hi, Lenny ...' Lenny (short for Leonora) has been our social worker since Mum first started fostering. Lenny's role is to support Mum irrespective of which child we've got. In fact, I've known Lenny for so long that sometimes she almost feels like an extra auntie or something.

I tried not to get too excited that Lenny was phoning us. She was probably just checking up on Mum because she knows how hard Mum always takes it after a foster-child leaves. She probably didn't have any news about Amy.

Then Mum blurted out, 'Oh, Lenny!' And she sat down heavily on the sofa.

'What's wrong, Mum?' I asked anxiously. 'Is it Amy? Is everything OK?'

Mum quickly told Lenny she would phone her back.

'Amy is fine. Lenny spoke to her social worker this afternoon,' she said. Her voice sounded shaky.

'Then what's wrong?' I demanded, because clearly something was.

'Nothing you need to worry about,' Mum told me. 'Now go and get ready – unless you want to go to Dad's in your school uniform.'

'But, Mum –'

'Poppy, you know I can't always tell you everything straight away. I need to talk more to Lenny first.'

'But –'

'Go and get ready – or I'll pack your bag myself and you'll just have to take what I choose to put in it.'

She always knows just what to say to motivate me.

*

I'm always especially choosy about my clothes when I'm going to stay with Dad. Unlike Mum, Dad is a really smart dresser and I want him to be proud of me. And the fact that I was about to meet his new – and probably very glamorous – girlfriend meant that I was even keener than usual to look my best.

As I got changed I suddenly remembered that I'd meant to wash my hair this evening so that it would be nice for the weekend. There was no time to do it now. I'd just have to do it at Dad's place.

Of course Mum had to walk in on me just as I was finishing getting ready. 'Poppy, what's taking you so long?' She frowned as she took in what I was wearing. 'Those jeans are far too tight across your bottom. Why on earth are you still wearing them when we got you those new ones last week?'

'Mu-um!' I moaned. Sometimes she *really* embarrasses me. 'They aren't that tight. Anyway, Dad said these ones make me look really slim cos they pull in my tummy.' I stood side-on to show her. 'See?'

'You don't need your tummy pulled in,' she said crossly. 'And your father's going to give you a complex about your shape if he doesn't stop making such thought-less comments.'

'It's not a thoughtless comment to say I look slim,' I protested. 'Dad told me that when he first met *you*, you were *really* slim. And he said your jeans were so tight you had to lie on the floor to do them up!'

Mum scowled. 'Poppy, I don't want *you* getting as hung up about your weight as I used to be when I was young. It made me very stressed and unhappy.'

'I know, Mum, and I'm not going to,' I said impatiently. Mum's told me countless times that outward appearance is only important up to a degree, and that it's *inner* beauty and being healthy that really count. And of course I know she's right. But still …

'Mum, I really want a new pair of glasses,' I said suddenly.

'There's nothing wrong with the pair you have, Poppy.' Mum sounded impatient because we'd had this conversation before. 'Besides, you only wear them in class.'

'So?' Sometimes Mum just doesn't seem to understand that school is one of the places where my appearance matters most.

'Poppy, if you didn't keep losing them or breaking them I wouldn't mind getting you another pair, but –'

'I only lost them once and broke them once,' I

34

protested. I was about to promise that in any case I would be more careful in future if she would only let me have another more attractive pair, when I looked out of the window and spotted Dad's brand new BMW parked across the end of our drive.

'He's here,' I said. As usual he didn't seem in any rush to get out of his car, and I guessed he was waiting for me to appear. The thing is, though he never admits it, I know he's just as keen as Mum to avoid having to make conversation with her on our front doorstep.

Chapter Five

'Poppy!' Dad greeted me warmly, giving me a kiss on each cheek as we met outside his car.

Dad is very different to Mum in lots of ways. If you can imagine someone who's very protective towards the people he loves, but also very stern and demanding at the same time, then that's my dad. Most people just see the stern and demanding part, plus they think he's posh because of the way he speaks. Dad comes from quite a wealthy family (though his father's business went bankrupt when he was in his early twenties) and he went to a pretty posh boarding school and then on to university to study law. He's always very knowledgeable and articulate about everything, which Mum says she used to love about him but now finds extremely irritating. And it's true that Dad always seems to find exactly the right words to complete his sentences, whereas Mum is always falling back on words like 'thingy' or 'doo-dah' or 'whatsitsname' to complete hers.

As he drove me to his place Dad asked me about my week, and since he's always super interested in anything to do with school I immediately launched into an account of our ill-fated science experiment. After that I found myself doing my best to find other particularly interesting or humorous things to tell him. Dad listened to me and made a couple of perceptive comments before I got the feeling that his attention was starting to drift. I stopped talking abruptly then, because the last thing I ever want to do is bore him. More than anything I want Dad to enjoy my company and to genuinely like me as a person, not just feel he has to put up with me because I'm his daughter.

The trouble is I know he thinks I take after Mum.

Don't get me wrong. It's not that I don't *want* to be like Mum. Mum is a really good person – not a *cool* person, but a good person definitely. The only reason that being like her is a problem is because even though Dad never talks about it, I know that at some point he must have stopped loving her. And I also know that even though he hardly spends any time with her these days, he still finds her highly irritating whenever he does. And the last thing I want is for him to find *me* irritating. Or worse still, for him to stop loving me.

'New jacket?' Dad asked as we pulled up at traffic lights.

Without thinking I answered, 'Yes! Mum found it in a charity shop.'

He scowled and I instantly realised my mistake. I'd forgotten to lie about the charity shop part. I quickly told him the name of the designer, hoping to impress him, but it clearly didn't even register.

'I pay your mother plenty of alimony,' he said gruffly, 'so I really don't understand why she finds it necessary to dress you in other people's cast-offs.'

'They're not cast-offs, Dad ...' I protested. 'Well, they *are*, I suppose ... but they're *vintage* cast-offs!'

He snorted like that was laughable. The trouble with Dad is that he just doesn't get the whole charity shop thing. He doesn't get that you can pick up some really great stuff, or that one person's cast-offs might be another person's treasure. For instance Mum loves finding retro clothes, especially Sixties or Seventies stuff, and she also loves absolutely anything (no matter how ugly or tacky) that reminds her of her grandparents' house when she was a kid. And I like finding unusual jewellery or scarves or bags to add to my accessories collection.

'Dad, don't you ever want to find yourself a bargain?' I tried hesitantly.

'I'm sure there are plenty of needier people than me out there who would benefit from snapping up a piece of decent second-hand clothing at a reasonable price,' he said. 'If people like your mother didn't go around creaming off all the best items, that is!'

'At least the money goes to a good cause,' I pointed out swiftly.

But Dad was still unimpressed. 'If you want to support a charity, then give them a monetary donation by all means. I still don't see why you should feel obliged to walk around in second-hand clothes!'

I opened my mouth to argue back, then decided I couldn't be bothered. I knew Dad would have the last word on the subject no matter what I said – after all, he is a barrister. Mum says it's the perfect job for him – getting to argue with people for a living. I know he loves his job so I think she's probably right.

'So, Poppy ...' Dad glanced sideways at me just as the traffic lights changed to green. 'About tomorrow ... I'll be introducing you to Kristen. Now while I do realise it can't be easy for you to see me with someone new –'

'Don't sweat it, Dad!' I interrupted with a little laugh. 'It's no biggie!' (After all, it had happened enough times before.)

He looked surprised at my response. 'Don't *sweat it*? No *biggie*? Is there some reason for the sudden deluge of slang, Poppy?' he demanded.

'Hey, I only used *two* slang expressions,' I defended myself. 'That's hardly a *deluge*.'

He looked even more surprised, and something else that I wasn't used to seeing – slightly amused and a little bit proud, maybe? He shook his head, muttering drily, 'You know, it's at times like these when I can definitely tell you're *my* daughter.'

And I'm ashamed to say that his comment pleased me far more than it should have.

Dad lives in an upmarket apartment block about a fifteen-minute drive from our house. His flat is on the fourth floor and it overlooks the river. It's got three bedrooms and two balconies. The smallest bedroom is mine whenever I stay there. Mum thinks he should have given me the second-largest bedroom because

40

it's not like he actually *needs* a home office since he puts in such long hours at work. But as I pointed out, since I only spend every second or third weekend at Dad's, I can see why he doesn't want to waste all that space.

When we got inside Dad ordered some Thai food. I'd never eaten Thai before and Dad always likes to introduce me to new things. (He thinks Mum doesn't do enough of that.)

We ate it while we watched a film together on his massive plasma screen. I mostly only ate the rice because the rest was too spicy, but I didn't mind. He never thinks any food he's bought me is a waste of money so long as I've actually tried it.

'What about your car, Dad?' I suddenly remembered. 'Don't you have to take it to the garage?'

'Oh, they phoned to cancel while I was on my way to collect you. Since I'd already changed the arrangement with your mother I thought I'd better stick to it.' He must have seen the look on my face because he added, 'What's wrong?'

'Nothing ... it's just ... I probably should have stayed with Mum tonight in that case. Amy left this morning and Mum's really missing her.'

Dad seemed slightly irritated as he replied, 'I shouldn't worry too much, Poppy. Your mother's had enough experience of saying goodbye to foster-children by now.' He paused, softening his voice a little as he added, 'Actually, *you're* the one I'm concerned about. You got rather attached to Amy, didn't you? I remember you even hoped your mother might adopt her.'

Unexpectedly my eyes pricked with tears. Dad surprises me sometimes with the things he remembers that I've said. 'Mum says we wouldn't have been the first choice as a forever family, but I still think if Mum had *wanted* to adopt her then social services might have let her. I mean, it took them ages to find the right family and by *that* time she was already part of *ours*.'

Dad looked thoughtful. 'You know, your mother's never given me a straight answer when I've asked what she actually *gets* out of all this fostering. Of course I understand that she's helping these children, but at what cost to you and herself? It's obviously painful to get so attached to these little girls, only to relinquish them again at the end of their time with you. Perhaps I should speak to her again about it.'

'No, Dad!' I felt like I'd betrayed Mum now that Dad was turning it into this sort of conversation. 'It's not

Mum's fault! We're supposed to remember we're not a forever family! With Amy I just forgot!'

'Sounds like it.'

I scowled. 'Yes, well, it won't happen again.'

'I see. And those sorts of feelings are something you have control over, are they?'

'Of course!' I found myself looking at him uncertainly. 'I mean … I must have, mustn't I?'

'Well, what do *you* think, Poppy?' He was using his don't-expect-me-to-spoon-feed-you-the-answer voice.

'I don't know,' I told him stubbornly.

'If I were you, Poppy, I'd give it some thought and see what you come up with,' he advised me.

I scowled. Recently he's had this real thing about encouraging me to think for myself rather than just 'absorbing other people's opinions like a sponge', as he puts it. OK so I can see why he does it, but frankly there are times when I just wish he'd let me do the sponge thing.

Just before I went to bed that night Dad reminded me he'd be in the swimming pool first thing tomorrow morning – the one in the basement of his apartment block – and he asked if I wanted to join him. I shook my head since I never like going swimming with Dad. He always swims endless lengths and encourages me to do the same and I always feel really pressured.

'So when do I get to meet Kristen?' I asked.

'We're meeting her in the cafe in the park tomorrow morning.' He paused. 'You know, she's very nice, Poppy. I'm sure you'll get along.'

'Nice?' I repeated with a smirk. That isn't a word my super-articulate dad uses very often.

He frowned slightly. 'I was trying to say that she's easy to talk to. She's got a very friendly manner. Everybody likes her.'

'Not like Penelope, then,' I said before I could stop myself. '*She* was impossible to talk to – unless you'd been to boarding school like her and rode horses.'

Dad frowned. 'Don't stereotype people, Poppy.'

'I'm not. I'm just saying that I really hope Kristen isn't the same *type* as Penelope, that's all!'

Chapter Six

Dad and I walked to the park together the next morning and I noticed a couple of youngish women taking a second look at him as they passed us. Dad is pretty good-looking for a man in his late forties, I guess, especially when he's made as much of an effort as he had today.

'By the way, Poppy,' he began as we walked along. 'What's happening with the school council these days? You don't talk about it much.'

I remembered how I'd agreed to apply for that school council post just to please my father. It had never entered my head that I'd be shortlisted. But Dad had checked my proposal letter and made me rewrite it four times, thus ensuring I made it to the next stage. He had then insisted on helping me with my election speech. He hadn't written it for me but he had made me rewrite and then fine-tune that speech until it was perfect. And finally he had listened to me rehearsing it and coached me until I was delivering it with confidence. It had been pretty nice to get all that attention from him, actually. And to feel his pride in me when I told him I'd been given the job.

Though in retrospect I wasn't sure that any amount of positive attention made up for all the hassle the job entailed.

'Oh, well … we're helping to organise a whole school open day, for one thing,' I said. 'There'll be art exhibitions and science demonstrations and stuff like that.'

'That sounds good.'

'Actually it's a bit of a pain. And it's embarrassing having to make announcements about it to the other Year Eights.'

'Well, it's good to do something outside your comfort zone when you get the chance. You're a very capable girl, Poppy, but I still think you're far too cautious. And as my father used to say, the right amount of caution will stop you getting hurt, but too much will stop you getting anywhere.'

'Did he say that before or after he went bankrupt?'

He looked taken aback, I guess because I wouldn't normally answer him back like that. I wasn't sure why I was doing it except that I felt unusually ... well ... moody and mouthy (to put it bluntly).

Luckily his phone pinged at that moment. Kristen had sent him a text to tell him she was running late and that we should go ahead and start brunch without her.

Maybe she won't come at all, I thought. Though the weird thing was that I couldn't work out whether that would be more of a relief or a disappointment.

Half an hour later Dad and I were eating bacon buns and I was doing my best to be polite and not take my bad mood out on him. I was about to tell him he'd got a spot of tomato ketchup on his chin when an attractive young woman came up behind him and put her hand on his shoulder. She was slim and pretty with shoulder-length blonde hair and very striking green eyes. *No prizes for guessing who this is*, I thought.

'Kristen!' Dad immediately shoved his chair back and leapt to his feet to kiss her on both cheeks. 'I wasn't expecting you yet.'

She smiled. Luckily the smear of ketchup on his chin hadn't transferred to her face. 'I finished earlier than I expected.' She had a faint lilting accent I couldn't quite place. Irish, maybe? Scottish?

Ever the gentleman, Dad pulled out a chair for her,

inadvertently bumping it into the table leg and making his coffee spill. It struck me that I'd never seen him this clumsy before.

'Oops ...' He deftly cleaned up the spillage with a paper napkin. 'Kristen, what can I get you?' he asked.

'Don't worry, Peter. I'll go and get something in a minute – you go back to your bacon butty.' She was smiling at me now. 'So ... you must be Poppy?'

At that point Dad suddenly remembered he was supposed to be introducing the two of us. 'Oh, excuse me ... Kristen, this is of course my daughter, Poppy ... Poppy, this is Kristen ...'

Unfortunately I had just taken a large bite of bacon bun and now my throat seemed to close over as I tried to swallow it and speak at the same time. I started to choke. I picked up one of the paper napkins and held it over my mouth as Kristen came behind me and thumped my back. I spat out the food rather spectacularly in my napkin before lifting my head and giving them a sheepish look. 'Sorry.'

Dad was giving me an exasperated glare.

'That's OK,' Kristen said. 'Better that than have you choke on it!' She smiled at Dad. 'I think I'll just go and order something. I'll be back in a minute.'

As soon as she was gone I saw that Dad's face had gone really pink. 'Really, Poppy!' he admonished me.

'I *said* sorry.' I went over to deposit the napkin and its contents in the bin. On my way back to our table I picked up another one to give to Dad. '*You've* got a big blob of ketchup on your chin, by the way,' I told him. 'Hold still. I'll get it.'

Kristen must have been watching us from the counter because as she arrived back a few minutes later she smiled and said, 'Giving your dad a spit bath, eh, Poppy?'

I looked at her in surprise as she grinned mischievously. She was nothing like Penelope, I realised with relief.

Kristen began to ask me questions while she waited for her bacon roll to be brought to our table. I tried to work out if she was just pretending to be this interested in me to please Dad, but it didn't seem that way. It seemed like she genuinely wanted to get to know me. She also complimented my jacket and when I told her where Mum had bought it she didn't bat an eyelid. In fact, she asked me exactly where that particular charity shop was and said that she'd have to pop in sometime.

'It's good you like charity shops too,' I said, giving Dad a pointed look. 'A lot of people really don't get the whole "pre-loved" thing.'

As the three of us were walking out of the cafe together my phone rang. 'It's Mum,' I told them.

Dad nodded. Mum usually phones at least a couple of times to check up on me while I'm with him. 'Kristen and I will be over there feeding the ducks.'

'Feeding the – ?' I watched them walk over to the duck pond as Kristen took a bag of bread out of her bag. *This is different*, I thought, because Dad's never exactly been a duck-feeding, swing-pushing kind of father.

'Poppy, darling … are you OK?' Mum's voice sounded a bit strained at the other end of the phone.

'Yes, Mum. I've just met Kristen.'

'Oh … Is she like we thought?'

'Well … sort of …' I didn't want to lie, but I didn't want to tell Mum the truth either. I knew I'd hurt her feelings if I told her that although she *looked* just how we'd imagined her, this was the first one of Dad's girl-friends who I *hadn't* hated as soon as she'd opened her mouth. 'Mum, I can't really talk about it now,' I said quickly.

'Of course, darling. Now then … the reason I'm phoning is … well … is there any chance you can get Dad to bring you back in an hour or so?'

'Why? Has something happened?' I asked anxiously.

'No ... well ... nothing to worry about ... just something I need to discuss with you rather urgently and not over the phone. Can you ask him, please?'

'Sure, Mum. I'll text you back, OK?'

I came off the phone trying to guess what it was Mum needed to discuss with me. Could it be something to do with Amy? None of our foster-kids had ever come back to us after going to live with their adoptive parents, but I guess there's always a first time. Though if it was that, then why couldn't she just tell me on the phone? The more I thought about it, the more I thought it must be something bad. After all, why else would she want to actually be there with me in person when she told me? That set me off worrying and I knew I had to get home as soon as possible to find out what was going on. I hurried over to the pond, where Dad was teasing Kristen about her bread, telling her it was too good for the ducks.

'Poppy, does he *really* make you eat bread this stale?' Kristen asked as I joined them.

'He only ever chucks it if there's actual mould on it,' I joked. 'Listen, Dad ... Mum really needs me to go home now.'

'*Now?* Why?'

'She says she needs to discuss something urgently.'

'So why can't she discuss it on the phone?'

'I think something's happened that she thinks will upset me. Please, Dad, I want to go now.'

I knew he'd take me because right from when I was little we've had an agreement that if I ever want to go home to Mum while I'm with him, then he has to let me. (That's how he got me to agree to stay the night with him in the first place, back when I was much younger and really clingy to Mum.)

He gave an exasperated sigh and hurled his chunk of bread at the nearest duck with a bit more force than was necessary. 'Come on, then,' he said impatiently, raising his eyes heavenwards at Kristen when he thought I wasn't looking. 'Let's go and get your stuff.'

Chapter Seven

When I got home an hour later, Mum seemed very relieved to see me. I couldn't help thinking how much older and more weary she looked compared with Kristen. After Dad had driven off she closed the front door and let out a sigh. 'Poppy ... something's happened ...'

I knew at once that it must be important because she didn't even ask me about Kristen.

She told me that social services had contacted her this morning asking her to take in another foster-kid – one who needed to be moved today.

'Oh.' I tried to hide my disappointment that Amy clearly wasn't coming back to us.

'Only this time it won't be an official fostering arrangement,' she continued. 'The girl they want me to look after isn't in the care system yet and they're trying to avoid going down that route by placing her with a family member.' She paused. 'It's Sadie.'

'*Sadie?*' I felt like someone just punched me.

'Her father hasn't been able to look after her for several weeks so she'd been living with a friend of his. That's why she changed schools. But that placement has just broken down. That's why they've come to me ...' She frowned. 'Poppy, I can't just let her go into care.'

'I thought you said you wanted to *discuss* it – not that you've already decided!' I snapped.

'I meant I wanted time to *explain* it to you before Sadie just turns up. Her social worker is bringing her later this afternoon.'

'*What?*' My throat suddenly had a hard lump in it. *No, no, no ... this could not be happening.* 'But *why?*' I demanded. 'I don't understand. Where's her dad?'

'He got sent to prison two months ago.'

'Prison?' I gaped at her in disbelief.

'For fraud,' Mum added swiftly. 'I didn't know about it until today.'

Apparently Sadie's father – who Mum had told me before was an accountant – had been caught stealing large sums of money from his employers. He had been sent to prison for five years. 'Hopefully he'll get paroled before then, but in the meantime someone has to take care of Sadie,' Mum explained. 'Her father's friend kicked her out after an incident at her house last night and Sadie's dad asked social services to contact me.'

'But you haven't seen Sadie since she was tiny,' I protested. 'You don't even *know* her any more!'

'I know – and that is something I deeply regret. This is my chance to finally put that right.'

'Mum, there's nothing to *put* right! It's not *your* fault her mum ran away and her dad wouldn't let you stay in touch with her afterwards!'

Mum sighed. 'If I had dealt with things better ten years ago it might not have happened like that. I've always blamed myself for not handling things differently with Sadie's father.'

'But like you said, that was ten years ago, Mum. Why do you have to get involved *now*? It's got nothing to do with us any more!'

'Poppy, how can you say that?' Mum said sharply. 'It has everything to do with us. The poor child has no other relatives.'

'I DON'T CARE!' I shouted. 'And she's NOT a poor child!'

Mum looked shocked as I stomped out of the room.

Up in my bedroom I flung myself on my bed, aware of my heart racing. *How could she do this to me?*

Of course Mum followed me straight up the stairs. She always does that whenever we have a row and I've gone storming off. She never seems to think I need a cooling-off period and sometimes – like today – I really badly *do*.

As soon as she stepped in my room I yelled, 'You're so gullible, Mum! Can't you see he's just using you?'

'So what if he is? If it helps Sadie I don't mind.'

'Well, *I* mind! Mum, you don't even know what she's like!'

Mum frowned. 'What if I was the one in prison and Dad wasn't here to look after you? What if *you* had no one to turn to? How would you feel?'

I just snorted because that would never happen and she knew it.

'Poppy, she's my niece. Do you really expect me to just turn my back on her?'

I had no reply to that. I was eight when I found out about my cousin. Mum told me after I'd come across some photos of Mum with me as a baby, sitting next to a younger woman (who looked a bit like Mum) also holding a baby. A young man was standing behind them smiling.

Mum had told me the woman was her younger sister, Kim, the man was Kim's husband, Kevin, and that their baby daughter, Sadie, had been born two months after me. Of course I had been instantly full of questions, and Mum had explained it all patiently.

When Sadie was only two years old, Kim had met another man and had left Sadie and her dad to go away with him. The family hadn't even been able to find out where she'd gone. She'd eventually written to Mum saying she'd started a new life abroad and that she wasn't coming back. Mum had tried to help out with Sadie as much as she could, but since she and Kevin had never got on it hadn't been easy. Eventually they'd had a massive row and after that Kevin refused to have anything to do with us, even though he and Sadie still lived in the same town. Mum hadn't seen her since.

'You know, I always thought Kevin was a dodgy character,' Mum continued now, 'just not on this sort of scale. Your dad never liked him. *He* always said he understood why Kim left him, just not why she didn't take Sadie with her. Mind you, Kim was as selfish and irresponsible as they come. She caused my parents so much stress before they died. In fact, after your poor grandma had her nervous breakdown, Kim more or less did as she liked.

She ran away a lot as a teenager. She'd reappear when she ran out of money or fell out with her friends. It broke their hearts. And then leaving little Sadie – I don't know how she could do it. It's as if she didn't want to grow up.'

'It sounds as if Sadie's just like her!' I said as tears welled in my eyes. 'Don't try to make me feel sorry for her. You don't know her like I do, Mum! It's bad enough having her in my class at school …'

Mum looked a bit contrite. 'Darling, she's only going to stay with us on a temporary basis to start with. Social services will need to approve the placement in any case.' She paused. 'But for the moment we're her only relatives, and if she comes to us she can continue at the same school … Poppy, she's already lost her home and the only parent she's known. All I'm asking is for you to give her a chance.'

She didn't have to say anything else. I knew that nothing I could say or do would make her change her mind. Plus I suppose a part of me had started to feel just a tiny bit sorry for Sadie.

And after all, it wasn't like this was going to be a forever placement.

Chapter Eight

Later that afternoon when the doorbell rang I stayed in my room. 'Poppy, please try and be welcoming,' Mum had said. 'I know the two of you haven't hit it off at school, but she really needs our help.'

I had promised to do my best, but I was still dreading it.

After a while I heard the social worker who had brought her leave. Then the house seemed very quiet. I imagined Mum stuck in the kitchen not knowing what to do, while Sadie sat silently glaring daggers at her. Mum is brilliant with all stroppy, needy little kids, but this was different. I doubted she'd have the first clue how to handle a moody Sadie.

I forced myself to get off my bed because, like it or not, I was beginning to worry a bit about Mum. The least I could do was go downstairs and check she was OK. After all, despite all my stories about her from school,

Mum couldn't know what Sadie was really like now. I'd pointed her out to Mum a couple of times at school but Mum had been too nervous to approach her. Especially as Sadie had made it perfectly clear that she wanted nothing to do with us.

I walked into the kitchen to find Mum preparing a vegetable lasagne. She seemed surprisingly relaxed and there was no sign of Sadie.

'Poppy – there you are!' Mum said. 'Now, darling … I know all this must have come as a shock, but –'

'Where is she?' I interrupted sharply.

'She went to the loo. She'll be back in a minute.'

I heard footsteps behind me and turned to see Sadie standing in the doorway. She was wearing jeans and a stripy red-and-white sweatshirt. It was the first time I'd seen her out of school uniform and she looked older and prettier. Her hair was especially sleek and shiny, as if it had just been washed.

'Hi, Poppy!' she exclaimed, sounding pleased to see me.

I just stared at her. What was she playing at?

Mum was smiling at her. 'Did you find the loo, Sadie?'

I inwardly cringed as I waited for Sadie to give a sarcastic reply like, 'No, I just peed on the floor' or 'Yeah, like it's *so* hard to find because this is *such* a big house.'

I was shocked when she just smiled sweetly at Mum and said, 'Yes, thanks. I like that dolly loo-roll-cover thingy.'

Mum laughed. 'Really? I got it from a charity shop for 50p. It's just like the one my gran had when I was a child. Poppy hates it, don't you, Pops?'

I scowled, wanting to tell Sadie to stop sucking up to my mum. There was no way she *really* liked that thing.

'Of course you two already know each other –' Mum began.

'Yes, though we haven't told anyone at school that we're cousins,' Sadie interrupted politely. 'It seemed better that way, didn't it, Poppy?' Before I could respond she put on an angelic smile, adding, 'Anyway, thanks for letting me stay here. Otherwise I don't know what would have happened to me. I was scared in case I ended up in some awful children's home ...'

I scowled, not at all affected by her 'Poor Little Orphan Annie' speech. Everyone knew that Sadie Shaw was as hard as nails and as tough as they come. Still ... I supposed she might feel a little bit vulnerable not having her parents around any more, even if they *were* pretty useless.

'We were glad to help,' Mum answered, her voice oozing sympathy. 'Weren't we, Poppy?'

I nodded just to satisfy Mum. I knew Sadie was well aware that I wasn't really the least bit glad.

'Hey, is that a veggie pasta you're making?' Sadie asked Mum.

'It's vegetarian lasagne.'

'Yum!' Sadie looked genuinely pleased, almost as if she hadn't expected Mum to make any special effort just for her.

'Aren't you going to ask Mum if she used vegetarian cheese?' I asked.

'Of course I did, Poppy!' Mum answered, giving me a stern frown to warn me to stop stirring.

'Linda ... who I was staying with ... she *never* remembered to get vegetarian cheese,' Sadie confided. 'She thought me being a vegetarian was a massive pain.'

'Oh, I'm sure she didn't, Sadie,' Mum said.

'Yes she did – she told me so herself.'

'So, your social worker said that Linda was a long-standing friend of your dad ... is that right?'

'More like a long-standing on-off girlfriend really, but yeah ...'

Mum just nodded as if she'd suspected as much. 'But she's never actually lived with you and your dad?'

'Crikey, no! Though they've been on holiday together

a few times. I always stayed at my mate Alison's place when they were away.'

Mum nodded again. 'Poppy, will you please take Sadie upstairs now and show her where everything is?'

Thanks a lot, Mum, I thought. *Just what I wanted – time on my own with Sadie.*

As soon as we were out of earshot Sadie said sarcastically, 'There's no need to look so shocked, you know. It's not like you aren't used to having other people's kids dumped on you!'

I gritted my teeth. How did *she* know what I was used to? But at least I was seeing the normal Sadie now that we were on our own. Which at least proved that I was right about her and that I wasn't going completely crazy.

'I can't believe you even wanted to come here,' I whispered.

'Why not? Your mum's really sweet. In fact, she's a massive improvement on Linda. Shame I have to put up with *you* as part of the package!'

I didn't respond. I knew she was trying to wind me up and I was determined not to let her.

Her phone beeped and she paused to check who it was. I couldn't help seeing her screensaver – a photo of her with her arm around another girl, both of them pulling silly faces at the camera. Sadie was smiling as she read her text. 'It's Alison. Telling me to keep my chin up!'

My curiosity got the better of me. 'Is that her?' I pointed to the picture on her phone.

'Yeah,' she grunted.

She swiftly sent a text back before following me the rest of the way upstairs.

'Nice room,' she commented when I opened the door to Amy's bedroom … the spare bedroom now. She took in the pictures on the walls and the toys and books on the shelves and said, 'You usually take in much younger kids, right?'

'Yes,' I said coolly.

'Oh well, no matter. Your mum'll just have to change the decor.' She flung down her bag and sat on the bed, bouncing on it like she was testing out the mattress. 'Not bad,' she declared with a grin. 'I'll give it an eight out of ten. Have to take off a couple marks if lots of little kids have been sleeping here. It's bound to have been peed on loads of times, right?'

I felt my face going warm. 'We always have a water-proof cover on the mattress. It's probably still there.'

'That'll have to come off. They make you sweaty, plus I don't wee in the bed.'

'That's good to know,' I snapped.

'Oooh!' She let out a little laugh. 'Sarcastic, eh? You know what, Poppy? I've got a feeling you're not nearly as angelic as you make out.'

I shook my head at her. 'I just can't believe you're my cousin.'

'Ditto. My mates are going to have a hard time believing I'm related to such a dork.'

'You mean those kids you were with after school yesterday?' I had to admit I was curious about them. 'Hey, this "incident" last night that got you kicked out of your last place? Were *they* the ones involved?'

She touched the side of her nose to warn me to mind my own business. 'Maybe I'll introduce you sometime, now that we're going to be sisters.'

'We are *not*!' I protested. 'You're only here on a short-term basis.'

'Is that what your mum told you?' Her eyes were sparkling wickedly. 'Funny ...'

And she stood up and backed me out of her room, shutting the door firmly in my face before I could ask her what she meant.

Chapter Nine

After Sadie had been with us for a few days I started to get a really bad feeling about this whole arrangement. We'd done some emergency foster care before and it had usually been a matter of days before a new placement was being discussed. Even if one hadn't been available immediately, the social worker had been in touch a lot and there had been a very temporary feeling about the whole thing.

But it didn't feel like that with Sadie. Yes, a social worker had phoned, and Lenny had been round to talk to Mum, but nobody seemed in any great hurry to find Sadie somewhere else to go. The suitability of our home as an emergency placement had already been established as far as I could work out. So why was Mum planning dates for future social work visits and talking with Lenny about giving Sadie time to settle in?

We didn't tell anyone at school that she was staying with me, or that we were related. In fact, if anything we were interacting even less at school than we had previously. Some of the teachers knew of course, but they were keeping it to themselves. I certainly wasn't going to tell Anne-Marie since I knew she'd never be able to keep it a secret. I did eventually tell Josh, who promised not to tell anyone until I said he could, and I knew I could trust him to keep his word. I'd been worried that he'd be cross because I hadn't told him before about Sadie being my cousin, but he was cool about it.

'It's OK. You didn't want to talk about it. I get it. Though it's not as cool as the hitman story, is it?'

'Hey, I'd much rather have an uncle who's a crooked accountant than a hitman!' I joked. But I was relieved he wasn't angry with me. Maybe boys are different that way, or maybe it's just Josh. But if the situation was reversed I know *I'd* be pretty miffed!

I came home from school ahead of Sadie on Wednesday and took the opportunity to talk to Mum.

'Listen, you do realise Sadie's only showing you her best behaviour at the moment, don't you? What you're seeing is so *not* the real her! And you did tell her this is only temporary, didn't you?'

Mum stood up after putting a vegetable casserole in the oven and gave me her full attention. 'Stop worrying so much. I think everything is going very well under the circumstances.'

'But you've got to see that all this being super nice to you and complimenting you on your cooking and saying she likes that stupid loo roll cover … it's all fake!'

'Poppy, there's always a honeymoon period at the start of every new placement, and I'm not expecting this to be any different.'

I sighed. 'Mum, this isn't the same thing.'

'Of course it is!'

I shook my head and sighed again. Most of our foster-kids are perfectly behaved little angels when they first arrive because they're desperate for us to like them. With Amy that lasted about three weeks. This is what Mum means when she talks about the 'honeymoon period'. Sooner or later though, that always changes. In fact, quite often they go to the other extreme. The best way I can explain it is to repeat what Mum and Lenny told me after Amy crayoned all over my bedroom walls one day while I was at school. They said that most children who get taken into care have already lost at least one home and family, so as soon as they start to feel safe in a new one, they worry about losing *that* as well. So without really being conscious of why they're doing it, they begin to test just how 'safe' their new home is by misbehaving to see if they get kicked out. And often they'll keep testing us in different ways for quite a while.

'I really don't think this is the same,' I insisted with a frown.

'How do you mean?'

'It's just more ... I don't know ... more *manipulative* than that, like she really knows what she's doing.'

Before Mum could respond we heard the front door opening, and moments later Sadie was calling out a hello from the hall.

'I'm just going up to my room to start my homework,' she told Mum as she briefly stuck her head into the kitchen. 'By the way, Poppy says you're going to buy me new curtains but I think the curtains in my room are super cute. Did you really make them yourself?'

I rolled my eyes at her blatant sucking-up. The curtains in that room have got teddies on them so Amy had really liked them, but the seams are coming unstitched and they don't quite hang right because they were the first thing Mum made at a sewing class she went to a long time ago.

Mum just smiled and thanked Sadie for her compliment.

'Do you want me to set the table or something before I go?' Sadie asked sweetly.

I pulled a face, not that I let Mum see it. Honestly, the more helpful Sadie got, the more I wanted to hit her.

'So, Sadie, how do you like your new school?' Mum asked as the three of us sat down at the table an hour or so later. 'Are you settling in OK?'

'I guess so. The kids there aren't as streetwise as I'm used to. Still, I guess that'll help keep me out of trouble!'

She laughed and Mum joined in. I scowled and stabbed my fork extra hard into my dinner. 'I'm getting a bit sick of vegetables,' I said, but neither of them responded.

'The art facilities are fantastic!' Sadie went on, and I saw her smirking as she glanced around at the various childish paintings and pictures I'd done over the years, which Mum still insists on keeping up in the kitchen.

For the first time I noticed the gaps on the fridge door where Mum had taken down Amy's pictures so she could take them away with her. Mum had kept only two – a funny self-portrait and a scribbly one Amy had drawn of me. Beside them Mum had stuck our copy of Amy's most recent nursery school photograph, where she was smiling happily, her black curly hair tied in pigtails with two yellow ribbons.

Sadie had a funny look on her face as she gazed at a childish painting of daffodils I'd done for Mother's Day when I was six, that Mum had actually framed. For a moment I thought she looked jealous, but I told myself that was ridiculous. After all, why would Sadie be jealous of anything *I* had done, when she was easily the best artist in our year? In fact, she was probably one of the best artists in our school.

'Poppy tells me *you're* a very talented artist, Sadie,' Mum said as if she could read my mind.

'Oh yeah, well … it kind of runs in the family,' Sadie mumbled.

'Oh yes. I remember your dad used to be a very good painter.'

'He still is.' She sighed. 'I guess he's the one I get it from.' She looked at Mum a little shyly. 'Unless my mum … ?'

There was an uncomfortable pause.

Sadie's mum just wasn't talked about in such a casual way in our house.

Mum seemed to let out a breath she'd been holding. 'Oh no ... Kim was never the arty type,' she said. 'None of our family was very good at that sort of thing.'

There was another awkward silence as Sadie seemed to digest this information. It must be strange not to know such an ordinary thing about your own mother, I thought.

'Would *you* like to be an artist when you grow up, Sadie?' Mum asked, clearly trying to break the tension.

Sadie shrugged. 'Maybe ... If I'm good enough.'

'Oh, you're definitely good enough!' I put in before I could stop myself.

Mum looked pleased by my comment and I saw her glance at Sadie for some kind of response. But this time – maybe because I'd said something so unexpectedly nice – Sadie was struggling to find one.

Chapter Ten

The next few days passed and suddenly it was Saturday again. I couldn't believe Sadie had been staying with us for a whole week. I had avoided being alone with her as much as I could, and Sadie had continued to act like the perfect guest. Sadie's social worker had been and gone, seemingly perfectly happy with her temporary placement, and there was still no news about when she'd be moving on to a longer-term foster-family.

'How about we go out to the park for a bit, Poppy?' Sadie suggested as I came downstairs on Saturday morning. I'd already stayed in my room for longer than I normally would on a weekend morning because I was in no rush to join Sadie and Mum in the kitchen.

They'd actually been baking! The scones they'd made were already in the oven and now Sadie was busy loading the dishwasher. She was still wearing the pink flowery apron Mum had lent her.

I gaped at her in disbelief. 'What – you and me? Together?'

Sadie laughed. 'Yeah. The fresh air will be good for us, right?' She shot Mum her most open, butter-wouldn't-melt smile as she undid her apron.

Of course Mum fell for it. Mum is always saying I should get more fresh air. Fresh air is very good for your complexion apparently. So before I knew what was happening I was being sent out to the park with Sadie – the last person on earth I wanted to hang out with.

'You know what,' Sadie told me as soon as we left the house, 'I really like your mum. I think I'll start calling her "Auntie Kathy". And I don't think she's nearly as stuck-up as my dad made out.'

'She's not stuck-up at all,' I said crossly.

'Yeah, well, Dad says she used to be. He says she used to speak to him like he was the lowest of the low, and that she tried to interfere all the time in how he was looking after me after my mum left.'

'She was probably just trying to help, that's all.' I gritted my teeth. 'Like she is now.' I only just stopped myself from saying something cutting about Sadie's dad. Instead I asked, 'So when did you last see him?'

'I don't want to talk about it,' she said coldly.

'Fine,' I replied.

We walked on in silence.

'The park's this way,' I reminded her as she turned right instead of left at the bottom of our road.

'Look, we can split up now! You go to the park. I'll go where I'm going. I only suggested we go together so your mum wouldn't suspect anything. Linda always got uptight if I tried to go anywhere on my own.'

'Suspect *what*?' I demanded. 'Where *are* you going in any case?'

'Oh, you know ...' she answered in a sarcastic tone, 'it's Saturday, so that's the day I usually go and nick stuff from Sainsbury's.'

'Ha ha.'

'I'll meet you at the swings in two hours and then we can go back together. How's that?'

'I'm not hanging around in the park for two hours! Anyway, if you go off for that long I'll have to tell Mum.'

'Listen, Poppy, you know those mates you saw me with the other day? I'm going to meet up with them.

OK? And to be honest –' she looked me up and down witheringly – 'they're really not your kind of people. So the best thing you can do is cover for me with your mum – then my friends won't get mad at you and pay *you* a visit like they did Linda.'

'SADIE!' I yelled after her as she walked away, but she just ignored me.

As I watched her walk briskly towards the main road I wondered if I should tell Mum anyway. It wouldn't surprise me in the least if she really was going shoplifting. But I was a bit afraid Sadie might carry out her threat. I still didn't know what had happened at Linda's, but so far I'd been imagining all sorts of horrible stuff which I'd hate to have happen at ours: bricks through the windows, dog poo through the letter box, fire-setting, poisoning the cat. (OK, so *we* don't actually have a cat, but Tiger from next door is always lazing in the sun on our front doorstep.)

In the end I decided it was probably safer to let it go. Besides, what did I care if she went ahead and got into trouble? At least then Mum might see that I was right about her.

I took out my phone and called Josh, hoping he'd want to meet up for a bit. Thankfully he was also at a loose end and he agreed to meet me at the shops near the park.

'I'll meet you inside the gift shop,' I told him. 'You can help me choose a birthday present for my dad.'

'Oh no,' Josh complained. 'Do I have to?'

'See you in fifteen minutes,' I said with a grin, ending the call before he thought up a good enough excuse to back out.

Anne-Marie is always teasing me about Josh, referring to him as my boyfriend and asking me when the wedding's going to be. I keep telling her that we're just good friends, but she doesn't listen.

Recently I tried to shut her up by stating that I would never risk ruining my friendship with Josh by going out with him. But she even had an answer for that: 'That's silly,' she'd said. 'Because when you do get a boyfriend you won't be able to stay best friends anyway – your boyfriend will get jealous. Same thing will happen if Josh gets a girl-friend. So you might as well give the romance thing a go, because basically your friendship is doomed anyway.'

'Don't be too optimistic will you?' I'd said sarcastic-ally. 'Anyway, I don't even *want* a boyfriend. Not yet, at any rate!'

'What about what Josh wants?'

'I don't know. We've never discussed it.'

'Well, maybe you should.'

*

I arrived at the shops before Josh did. There's a little cafe there as well as the gift shop, a newsagent, an estate agent's and a second-hand bookshop.

I was inside the gift shop when Josh joined me. 'So let me guess … as per usual, you don't know what to get him?' he said when he found me standing in front of the men's toiletries with a big frown on my face. Like I said before, Josh has known me for a long time and he's well aware of how I'm always trying my hardest to impress my dad.

'Got it in one,' I murmured gloomily. 'It's this Friday.'

The trouble is I always get stressed about buying Dad's present, which Mum says is my own fault because I try too hard to get it perfect. She says not to worry because Dad will like anything I give him just because it's from me, but I'm not so sure that's true. I mean, he never wears the tie I gave him last Christmas, and the toiletries I bought him for his last birthday are still sitting on his bathroom shelf in their original packaging.

'I wish that just one time, I could get him something he really *loves*,' I confided in Josh. 'But it's hard because he has such expensive tastes in … well … in just about everything.'

Josh nodded sympathetically and started to follow me around the shop.

Once we were outside again (without buying anything) Josh said, 'What about the bookshop?'

I shook my head. 'He won't want anything from there.'

'I thought you said he doesn't do charity shops but he does do second-hand books?'

'Well, yes, but not the way Mum and I do them. Put it this way,' I said with a sigh. 'He won't want anything from in there that *I* can afford to buy him.'

Mum and I always spend ages in second-hand bookshops browsing the shelves to see what we can find and pausing frequently to show each other stuff or to read amusing blurbs out loud. Currently Mum is on a mission to replace all the children's books she remembers having as a girl.

Dad, on the other hand, makes straight for the locked glass cabinet behind the till where all the more valuable items are displayed. And if there's nothing there that interests him he just walks straight out again.

'What about going for nostalgic value instead?' Josh suggested, pointing at an old *Beano* annual in the window.

I shook my head at the *Beano* but I followed him inside anyway, not really expecting to find a present for

Dad, but knowing I'd have fun browsing for books Mum or I might like.

After a little while I spotted an old *Just William* hardback and I suddenly remembered Dad talking about how he used to like *Just William* as a boy. I picked up the book and showed it to Josh. 'But it's not signed and it's not a first edition or anything,' I said uncertainly.

'It doesn't matter. It's still a really original present. I know my dad would love it.'

'Yeah, but this is *my* dad we're talking about. He probably –' I broke off abruptly as someone I knew came into the shop. It was Josh's mate Sean from school.

Sean isn't as obviously handsome or as tall as Josh, but I suppose he's fairly good-looking in a boyish sort of way. And he's got really twinkly brown eyes. He's certainly very witty – another attribute Mum says she used to find super attractive in my dad, but now finds super irritating.

Now I remembered Josh telling me that Sean's mum worked in the estate agent's next door.

'Sean!' Josh immediately called out. 'What are *you* doing inside a bookshop? Oh … hi, Mr Anderson!'

Mr Anderson was right behind him. Like I said before, Sean's mum married our English teacher last summer. Apparently Mr Anderson is ten years younger than Sean's

mum, and Anne-Marie says that our teacher must therefore have some kind of 'mother complex' (whatever
that's supposed to mean). When I repeated it to Mum
she laughed and said that Sean's mum is really glamorous
and doesn't look like *anybody's* mother.

Anyway, I can't imagine anything more embarrassing
than having my mum marry a teacher in our school. Except
for everyone finding out my dad's in prison, perhaps.

Mr Anderson was smiling at Josh and me as he said,
'It's nice to see *some* of my pupils have developed a love
of reading, at any rate.'

'Poppy's thinking about getting this for her dad's birthday,' Josh told him, showing him my book. 'What do you
think? He used to read *Just William* when he was a kid.'

'Well, that sounds like an excellent choice, then,' Mr
Anderson replied, smiling kindly at me.

Sean was grinning at me cheekily. '*Your* dad sounds nice
and normal. *Leo* was reading the classics and reciting poetry
right from when he was in his pram, weren't you, Leo?'

Mr Anderson put an arm around his shoulder. 'Tell
you what, Sean. Let's find the poetry section and you can
choose a book for yourself while we're here. My treat!'

Sean laughed, while I just stood there feeling self-
conscious. It was so weird to see my hunky English

teacher in 'dad' mode – and it was also weird how much *less* hunky that seemed to make him.

'Come on, Poppy, let's get it,' Josh said, leading me towards the front of the shop to pay for my book.

Suddenly Sean whirled round. 'Wait a minute … I meant to congratulate you, Poppy.'

'Huh?'

'*Sean.*' Mr Anderson's voice held a warning which Sean clearly had no intention of heeding as a grin slowly began lighting up his face.

'What are you on about?' Even Josh sounded puzzled.

'Mum just told me the story this morning.' Sean started to laugh. 'Her and Leo have got this whole *Does my bum look big in this?* thing going on … and this morning Mum told me what started it. Way to go, Poppy! At least there's one girl in our school who doesn't think Leo's perfect!'

'Sean!' Mr Anderson sounded cross now, and maybe even a bit embarrassed.

As for me, embarrassed didn't even begin to cover it! I could feel myself flushing bright red and all I wanted was to find myself a deep, dark hole to bury myself in.

Chapter Eleven

Josh laughed all the way back to the park entrance.

'It's not funny, Josh!' I wailed. 'Next time I see Mr Anderson I think I'll die. In fact I just want to die *right now.*'

'Don't be daft! *He* obviously thought it was funny or he wouldn't have gone home and told his wife, would he?'

Josh was still struggling to contain his mirth when we reached the park.

'Just go home, will you?' I snapped.

'OK, OK ... But it's no big deal. Just chill ...' I could still hear him laughing as he walked away.

I entered the park alone. I was fuming. This was all Anne-Marie's fault for blabbing as usual. Maybe Olivia was right. Maybe I should just dump her completely as a friend. It might be a lot safer that way. If only Olivia was still here, I thought.

Since there was no sign of Sadie yet I sat down on the nearest bench and took out *Just William* to have a proper look at it. One of the things I love about old books is the illustrations, and this one had some beauties. I just hoped Dad didn't think it was a really naff present, that's all.

I'm not sure how long I'd been sitting there reading when someone suddenly appeared behind me and grabbed the book. It was Sadie.

'What's this, then?' She was grinning as she bent the front and back boards back so that all the pages in between splayed out like a fan.

'Watch it. You'll break the spine,' I said angrily.

'So? It's not like it can feel it, is it?' She chucked it back at me.

'Where've you been?' I demanded, standing up and glaring.

'Over at my best mate Alison's place. Don't tell your mum unless you want that book of yours to need some major spinal surgery!' She laughed like she thought she was being super witty.

'I thought you were going to see those mates from the other day? The ones who were at the bus stop with you?'

'Yeah … I did!'

'You mean Alison's one of *them*?'

'Yeah.'

'But they were much older than you!'

'Alison's seventeen. Nearly eighteen actually.'

'But …' I had a sudden alarming thought. 'She wasn't the girl who was hitting you, was she?'

'Hitting me? Oh yeah, I remember. She was mad because I was really late getting there and she'd had to go off looking for me.'

'But how can *she* be your friend?'

'She calls me her adopted kid sister! She always looks out for me. We lived in the same road for ages. *Her* mum went off with some other bloke too, so once she knew I was in the same boat she sort of took me under her wing.'

I guess I could understand that. 'But she shouldn't hit you!' I insisted.

'Oh … that was just a few smacks because I nearly made us late for Joe. He'd borrowed his brother's car to pick us up.'

'Who's Joe?'

'Alison's boyfriend.'

'And does *he* hit you too?'

'Of course not! Alison wouldn't let him!'

'Well, *she* shouldn't either. It's bullying!'

'Poppy, why are you getting so worked up? She'd

never really hurt me. And she'd never let anyone else hurt me either. That's not the problem!'

'Oh? So what *is*?'

She stayed silent, but just as I thought she'd completely clammed up she asked, 'Poppy, have you ever been forced to make a really hard decision? To make a choice that you really don't want to make?'

'Well …' I thought about it. 'I had this best friend called Olivia last year. Anne-Marie was my best friend too. But Anne-Marie said I couldn't have two best friends and that I'd have to choose.'

Sadie seemed to find that amusing. 'I've noticed Anne-Marie is pretty possessive. So what did you do?'

'I chose Olivia. Then she moved away in the summer.'

Sadie snorted. 'I bet you felt like a right klutz! Talk about backing the wrong horse!' She was enjoying this way too much now.

'Shut up, Sadie,' I snapped. 'So what's *your* big decision, then?'

Before she could answer her phone beeped and she swiftly checked her text. 'It's Alison. She went to the cafe to get us some hot chocolates while I came to fetch you. She's waiting for us at the gate.'

'What? You mean she's actually *here*? Wait a minute …'

But Sadie was already leading the way.

I followed behind her slowly, feeling nervous and curious both at the same time. I made sure I put my book safely away in my bag before I got to the gate.

Sure enough, there was the older girl I'd seen with Sadie at the bus stop. She wore jeans today and a denim jacket with different arty-looking patches sewn all over it. Her hair was still short and spiky and she wore big earrings and a nose stud. She was holding two polystyrene cups with plastic lids.

Sadie quickly introduced us. 'Alison, this is Poppy – my cousin.' I was quite surprised to hear her say that so readily after all the times at school when she'd acted like she didn't want anyone to know.

'Hey, Poppy.' Alison gave me a bit of a stare as she placed the two takeaway drinks on the wall beside her.

'Hi,' I mumbled nervously. 'Sadie's ... um ... told me about you.'

'Oh yeah? What did she say?'

'Um ... just that you're her friend.'

'*Best* friend,' Sadie corrected me crossly.

'More of a big sister, I'd say,' Alison corrected both of us. I wasn't expecting what happened next. She reached forward and gripped Sadie in a massive hug.

'Whatever you do, make sure you always leave your phone switched on. If I can't contact you I'm going to get really mad, OK?'

Sadie nodded. 'I promise.'

'OK. See you soon!' Alison picked up one of the cups and walked off down the street without looking back.

As we walked home together Sadie said, 'Remember – don't you dare start repeating *any* of my business to your mum or *anyone* else ...'

'Listen, Josh already knows you're my cousin,' I told her quickly. 'Our mums are really good friends and they tell each other everything. He knows about your dad, but there's no way he'd ever tell anyone.'

'He'd better not!' She sounded cross. 'Same goes for that gossipy Anne-Marie.'

'Anne-Marie doesn't know anything. But Sadie, you do realise there are already a few crazy rumours about you going around at school, don't you?'

'What rumours?' she demanded.

'It's just ... well ... some people are saying your dad's a ... a hitman,' I mumbled, feeling a bit stupid just repeating it. 'That's what Anne-Marie was about to say the other day. You know … when Mr Jamieson called you over … but listen, I don't want you thinking *I* started that rumour, or that Anne-Marie or Josh did, because –'

'Oh, but that's *brilliant*!' Sadie interrupted.

I frowned. 'It is?'

'Oh yes!' She was grinning. 'You see, a few weeks ago that nosy Julia saw me coming out of Mrs Thomson's room and asked why I was seeing the school counsellor. So I told her you *have* to see the school shrink if your dad's a hitman!'

'Oh!'

'I am *so* going to have fun with this!' She checked her watch. 'Come on. I'm starving. Let's go home and see what's for lunch.'

When we got there we found Mum sitting at the kitchen table sipping a mug of tea and studying her new vegetarian recipe book. Judging by the smell she had something already cooking in the oven. Sadie stuck her nose in the kitchen to say hello and comment on 'the delicious smell' before going off upstairs.

'Is Sadie all right?' Mum asked me. 'She looks tired.'

The concern in her voice really annoyed me. After all,

if Sadie was tired then she only had herself to blame. 'Yeah, well, I guess it must be pretty exhausting pretending to be nice all the time,' I snapped. 'Still – at least she gets a rest from that when she's with me.'

'Poppy …' Mum closed the book with a bang, patting the seat next to her. She fixed me with the look she always gives me when she doesn't think I'm being sympathetic enough to some other person's predicament. 'I think we need to have a talk, don't you?'

I sighed, and got myself a glass of water before sitting down next to her. I badly wanted to tell her how Sadie had sneaked off on her own today, but I was too scared after Sadie's threats. Still, that didn't mean I had to agree with her that Sadie was perfect.

'Mum, you have to see that she's not nearly as sweet and innocent as she's making out!' I hissed before she had a chance to start talking.

'Poppy, I've been through enough honeymoon periods with enough foster-children to know not to get complacent just because things are going well at this stage,' Mum assured me. 'I'm well aware that she'll start testing me sooner or later – just like they all do. Then I'm sure she won't be nearly so complimentary and well behaved, but until then –'

'Mum, this isn't the same! Sadie's deliberately manipulating you. Why can't you see that?'

Mum sighed. 'Poppy, she may be family, but at the end of the day she's in exactly the same position as all the other children we've taken in. She's been abandoned by the very people who are *meant* to love and protect her. And she doesn't trust that it won't happen again.'

'This is different, Mum! She's being super nice to you and horrible to me. None of the others did that.'

'Sadie is a lot older than they were. Maybe that has something to do with it.' She paused. 'You've always been so patient and kind with all the others, Poppy. Can't you just give Sadie the same chance you've given them?'

I frowned. I could see that Sadie had had it pretty rough until now, and it wasn't that I didn't think she deserved a chance. But Sadie wasn't being honest with Mum. And it wasn't fair that she was somehow managing to wedge herself in between Mum and me so that it felt like she was pushing us apart.

'Mum, what happened at Linda's on Friday night?' I asked nervously. I had to admit that my mind had been coming up with all sorts of horrible possibilities since Sadie had made her threats to do the same at our house.

'She hasn't told you?'

'No.'

Mum sighed. 'Apparently last year Linda inherited a lot of money from her great-aunt, and also some personal items – clothes, shoes, ornaments, crockery, jewellery, that sort of thing. Most of it was in her spare room waiting to be sorted out. While Linda was out last Friday evening, Sadie and some friends went into the spare room and went through it all, chucking things out of the window into the garden.'

'But that's … that's … *horrible*!' I exclaimed, imagining that happening to all my stuff.

Mum nodded. 'Linda came home just as they were about to set fire to it all. She called the police but in the end she decided not to press charges.'

'But *why*? I mean why did Sadie do it?'

'She wouldn't say, though things hadn't been going well between her and Linda for some time apparently. Anyway, Sadie is banned from seeing those friends from now on.'

'Banned? But –' I broke off, too scared now to tell Mum what I knew. 'But Mum, doesn't *this* show you what she's really like?' I pleaded. 'She did that to Linda after Linda took her in and tried to help her!' I paused. 'What if she gets her friends to do the same here?'

'You don't have to worry about that, Poppy,' Mum said at once. 'It sounds as though she and Linda had a very poor relationship and Linda was a very unsuitable choice of carer for her. Sadie's given me her word that nothing like that will happen here.'

'Sadie's word doesn't mean anything!' Frankly I felt almost as angry with Mum as I did with Sadie. How could she bring Sadie into our home after what she'd done? 'Mum, you *said* Sadie was only here on a trial basis, right?'

Mum nodded. 'Yes. We've agreed with her social worker that we'll wait and see if this trial period is a success before deciding on the next step.'

'But the next step is Sadie moving somewhere else, right?'

'Yes … well … before we decide that, I think it's worth waiting to see how well Sadie settles with *us* if we give it a bit more time.'

'WHAT?! Mum, NO! That's NOT what you said before!'

'Listen to me, Poppy … Lenny is going to speak to you about all of this before we decide anything. You'll have the chance to tell her all your concerns. But I want you to think hard about what you're going to say, because you know Lenny will take it seriously.'

'*Good!* At least *somebody* will!' I glared at her so hard that she actually looked a bit upset. I was glad. I couldn't believe she had tricked me like this. She'd said nothing before about there being any possibility of Sadie staying with us permanently.

'Poppy, think how *you'd* feel if it were you in Sadie's position …' Mum sounded almost like she was pleading with me. 'The poor child has no parents and *no* home of her own, whereas you've got here *and* your dad's place to fall back on.'

I looked at her in disbelief. Did she even realise what she'd said? 'So now I'm *lucky* to come from a broken home, am I?' I rasped.

'I didn't say that!'

'Yes you did! You know, maybe I *should* just go and live with Dad! Maybe that would solve the problem!'

'Poppy, I –'

But I didn't want to hear any more and I stormed upstairs, only to find Sadie standing in the doorway of her bedroom, a smug look on her face. She pushed her door shut when she saw me but I knew she had to have overheard.

Once I was alone in my bedroom I fully expected

Mum to follow me upstairs like she usually does when I stalk off like that. Only she didn't.

After a while another thought hit me. What if the reason she hadn't come after me was that she was busy thinking over what I'd suggested?

And what if she decided that me going to live with Dad was actually quite a good idea?

Chapter Twelve

I was quite glad to be going to school on Monday morning just to get away from Mum and Sadie. Even first thing, Sadie was all smiles and compliments about the way Mum made toast. Apparently Linda's toast was either too soggy or too well done, whereas Mum's was just perfect.

I hardly spoke to either of them at breakfast. I felt betrayed by Mum, and as for Sadie – well, it was all I could manage not to pick up my toast and throw it at her.

In the bathroom I saw Sadie had shoved some of the stuff on my shelf to one side and put out her own toiletries. Typical Sadie, not even asking before she did that.

'You know you're still only here on a trial basis, don't you?' I reminded her as I met her on the landing after I'd brushed my teeth. 'Nothing's been decided yet about whether or not you can stay longer.'

'Is that what you think?' Her eyes were sparkling wickedly.

'Yes.' I struggled to keep my cool. 'It's not even just up to us. Social services have to do an assessment first.'

'Sure, but if your mum's happy and I'm happy, they're not going to upset the apple cart, are they? And even if *you* kick up a fuss I have a feeling your mum's not going to listen.'

'Yes she will,' I snarled.

Sadie shrugged. 'It's just, she seems pretty pleased to be looking after me. Dad says that's what she wanted when I was little but he wouldn't let her have me. That's why they fell out.'

I glared at her. 'Yeah, right …'

Sadie just smiled like she knew better. 'Your mum needs people to need her,' she whispered. 'And I need her *more* than you do. After all, you've still got your dad, whereas I've got nobody. She won't kick *me* out.'

I realised she must have heard most of my argument with Mum last night. I suddenly remembered something Dad had once shouted at Mum when they'd been rowing – something I hadn't really understood at the time. He'd yelled that he was sorry he wasn't *needy* enough for her. Now for the first time I thought I understood what he meant. Mum was always helping out needy people. Maybe Sadie was right. Maybe if I tried to make Mum choose between Sadie and me then she *might* actually choose the one she thought needed her most.

But I wasn't about to let Sadie know how she'd got to me.

'She *will* kick you out when I get her to see what you're *really* like,' I retaliated.

Sadie just grinned. 'Well, good luck with that.'

As I walked to school alone I tried to think of something nice to occupy my mind – something that had nothing to do with Sadie. I started thinking about Amy and all the fun times we'd had together. But that just got me dwelling on the fact that Amy was the little sister I'd always wanted. If only Mum had adopted her! Mum was going on about how much Sadie needed us, but what about Amy? In the beginning, when Amy had no prospective parents lining up to adopt her, we were all *she* had. How come Mum hadn't felt so strongly about giving *her* a home?

The more I thought about it, the angrier I became with Mum.

I started thinking about Lenny's next visit and

everything I wanted to say to her about Sadie. But I knew I had to be careful. Even if I got Lenny to decide that Sadie and I couldn't live in the same house together, Mum might not want Sadie to leave. After all, whereas Sadie had nobody else to look after her, Mum knew I could always go and live with Dad as a backup.

The morning at school was OK, but straight after lunch we had double English, which meant I had to face Mr Anderson again after that whole embarrassing incident in the bookshop at the weekend.

To my surprise he actually came up to speak to me at my desk before Anne-Marie or Sadie arrived. 'Guess how Sean spent his Sunday afternoon,' he said in a quiet voice. 'Doing a book report on a *poetry* book! That'll teach him, huh?' He gave me a good-natured grin that clearly said 'No hard feelings', and even though I was starting to blush I was glad we had cleared the air.

I felt better until Anne-Marie joined me, gave me a sharp nudge and demanded to know why I hadn't told her that my mum was fostering Sadie. Word had clearly got out, though Anne-Marie didn't seem to know yet that Sadie was actually my cousin.

Five minutes before the bell was due to ring for

afternoon break, Mr Anderson said he'd like to hear a few of the poems we'd written for homework. We were supposed to read them out last Friday but there hadn't been enough time.

I hadn't even done mine. The trouble was I hadn't been able to find Anne-Marie's sketch, though she swore she had definitely put it in my bag. I didn't think Mr Anderson would mind that much as he always treats his last-thing-on-a-Friday-afternoon tasks as a bit of fun, but Anne-Marie was clearly pretty annoyed. She picked up my schoolbag to search inside it herself as someone on the other side of the room read out their poem.

The next person to be picked was Sadie.

She looked very calm as she stood up. 'I had Poppy's drawing,' she announced.

That's when I started to feel my heart thumping. Why had I given her my sketch of Amy? Now she was going to make fun of it …

I twisted round in my seat to look at her and it was all I could do not to turn back to face the front and plug my fingers in my ears.

'*AMY*,' she read out in a calm voice as she held up my picture. Her poem was very short and nothing like I'd expected.

'A is for Afro

M is for mischievous

Y is for yellow ribbons.'

Then she sat down in her seat abruptly.

I immediately thought of the photo on our fridge of Amy with yellow ribbons in her hair and a mischievous grin on her face. I have to say I felt a bit stunned.

'Very good, Sadie,' Mr Anderson said. 'Simple and very effective. Well done.'

'Trust her,' Anne-Marie hissed in my ear, though I knew she was just jealous that Sadie was getting praised and not her. 'That wasn't even a proper poem. At least the verse *I* wrote about her stupid bird is humorous and does actually rhyme!'

'Wait … you managed to write a *humorous* poem about a bird that's had its throat cut and then been stuffed?' I said. 'I thought you were an animal lover!'

'I am. I just did it to annoy Sadie. If I don't get picked to read it out I'm going to slip it into her bag.' She grinned. 'Probably safer to do that anyway!' She returned to rummaging in my bag, which she had half emptied out on to our desk.

'Found it!' she hissed as she pulled out her missing drawing. 'It was in your science folder. You didn't look very hard, did you?' She gave it to me and I saw that she'd drawn a man with a gigantic bum and written 'Mr Anderson' beside it.

'Anne-Marie, you are pathetic,' I whispered.

'What's this then, Poppy?' To my horror I realised Mr Anderson was coming up behind me.

'It's not mine,' I hissed, but I wasn't sure if he heard me as the bell rang to signal the end of the lesson. 'It's Anne-Marie's,' I added, but my voice was drowned out by everyone else's as they packed up their stuff ready to leave.

'Oh dear,' Mr Anderson said when he saw it. 'Thanks for that, girls. Please tell me you haven't got a poem to go with it.'

'No ... there's no poem,' we both said together.

I felt like my whole face had burst into flames as I left the classroom.

Anne-Marie was trying to stop giggling. 'Sorry,' she whispered. 'It was meant to be a joke. I didn't think he'd see it.'

'Well, he did!' I snarled. 'You do realise he's going to think I'm totally obsessed with the size of his bum now?'

But that just made her giggle even more.

*

I went over to the nearest bit of wall in the playground and sat down. I wished I could just run home and hide. If only I could hole up in my bedroom until I stopped feeling like I was … I don't know … leaking out my worries all over the place or something. It's hard to describe, but it felt like the invisible barrier that usually does a great job of containing all my thoughts and feelings had suddenly stopped working and the rest of the world could actually *see* the really uncool mess going on inside my brain.

'Are you OK, Poppy?' I turned to see Josh in full big-brother mode, looking all concerned as I bit my bottom lip and tried not to give in to the urge to bawl my eyes out.

'Not really,' I grunted.

'What's up?'

'Everything!' I told him about Anne-Marie's sketch, and I guess I shouldn't have been surprised when his first response was to laugh.

'Oh dear …' he spluttered, then pulled a straight face as he saw how close to tears I was. 'Listen, if you like, I'll get Sean to explain –'

'Sean?' I scoffed. 'Don't be stupid! He'll be too busy rolling about laughing to explain anything.'

'Not if he sees how upset you are.'

'Sure … *right.*'

'No, you'll see. Sean likes you. He's going to want to help. He's only gone to the tuck shop … there he is now …'

I felt myself flushing for absolutely no reason when Sean arrived and sat down on the wall beside us. He offered us his crisps and Josh took one.

'Listen, Sean … you know that mate of Poppy's with the big mouth – Anne-Marie? She's dropped Poppy in it with Leo and I was thinking you could help sort it,' Josh told him. (It was funny hearing Josh refer to our English teacher by his first name. He's started to do that quite a bit when he's with Sean.)

'Josh, leave it. It doesn't matter!'

'Anne-Marie drew an embarrassing picture of Leo and he saw Poppy with it,' Josh continued as if I hadn't spoken. 'Now he thinks Poppy drew it.'

'An embarrassing picture? Brilliant! Did it feature his enormous bum, by any chance?' Sean was grinning.

I felt my face getting even hotter. 'Josh – I told you to leave it!' I spat out angrily, jumping up to leave. But to my horror, before I could get away, I started to cry. (Sometimes when I'm really angry about something, it's like my brain has gone bananas and the angry bit has got cross-wired with the upset bit or something.)

'Hey!' A hand reached out and grabbed my arm. At first I thought it was Josh, and I was about to shake him off when I saw that the hand belonged to Sean. 'I'm sorry ...' he said. 'I should stop going on about it, but it was just so cool what you said that time, that's all ... you see all the other girls at school were going on endlessly about how perfect he is ... which makes you want to throw up after a while ... and there *you* were saying ... well ... you know ...'

I stood facing him, trying to assess if he was winding me up. His eyes were pretty sincere.

'Julia blew the whole thing way out of proportion,' I said through gritted teeth. 'I didn't even say it the way she made out.'

'Well, don't worry, cos you haven't given Leo a complex about his bum, if that's what's bothering you. He already knows he spends way too much time sitting on it reading books and that he needs to start cycling everywhere like Mr Christie if he wants to get a 5/5!'

'Anne-Marie was the one who invented that stupid quiz – not me!'

'I think he knows that, Poppy.'

'But now he's seen that horrible drawing Anne-Marie did and he thinks it's mine –'

'Don't worry about that. I bet he already guessed who did it. He's pretty smart about that kind of thing. But just in case, I promise I'll tell him it was Anne-Marie. OK?'

'Could you?' I asked hopefully. 'But be careful cos I don't want to get Anne-Marie into trouble and –'

'You know what? You're just like my sister!' he interrupted me with a cheeky grin. '*She's* always worrying and overthinking everything too!'

Chapter Thirteen

The next bit of trouble between Sadie and me started that afternoon when we got home from school. I'd had to explain to Anne-Marie why Sadie was living with us and I'd ended up telling her we were cousins. I had told her as few of the details as possible and asked her to keep it a secret, but Sadie was still furious because she said Anne-Marie would definitely blab and then it would be round the school in no time.

'It doesn't matter that much if they know, does it?' I defended myself.

'That's easy for you to say!' she huffed.

'What's that supposed to mean?'

'What do you think it means?'

'Listen, she was asking me loads of questions and I had to give her *something* or she'd never have shut up. Maybe I should've told her your dad's in prison instead?'

She glared at me angrily. 'You didn't have to tell her *anything*! Hey, what's *this*?'

She had been emptying out her schoolbag looking for her homework diary and she'd just discovered the poem Anne-Marie had put there earlier.

I once killed a bird
Whose last words were absurd –
'I'd be chuffed to be stuffed,' it did say.
So I said I would pay
To put it on display
And the taxidermist came the next day.

I laughed when Sadie showed it to me. It was actually one of Anne-Marie's better creations. In fact, I couldn't help wondering if her dad had helped her with it. He's a bit of a joker and I could imagine him encouraging her with something like this.

'It's not funny!' Sadie said angrily. 'People really do kill animals and birds just to get them stuffed.'

'Come on, Sadie,' I protested. 'Anne-Marie was just having a bit of fun. She's the last person who would hurt an animal. She's totally potty about them. Her whole back garden and conservatory are full of rabbit hutches and cages with gerbils and guinea pigs and hamsters and stuff. She gets them from rescue centres and looks after them all by herself, cleaning out their cages and using her pocket money to buy them things they need. I'm telling you she's animal mad.'

Sadie had gone alarmingly quiet. 'I had no idea,' she finally murmured.

'Well … yeah …' I was a little confused by her reaction.

'So it's a sort of zoo for small furries?'

'Well … sort of, I suppose …'

'I don't agree with zoos. Or with animals being kept locked up in cages.'

'Oh come on, Sadie, they're pets. They'd die in the wild.'

'Better to die in the wild than live in a cage for your whole life,' Sadie said.

'But they aren't in cages the whole time. The rabbits get the run of the garden and the guinea pigs have an outside run too. Anyway, they're domestic rabbits. They're meant to be kept as pets.'

'Alison says a cage is a cage however you try and dress it up,' she stated firmly.

'She *would*,' I muttered.

'Did I tell you she got expelled from school last year for trashing the science lab?' she added proudly. 'It was a protest because she found out our science teacher used to work in a laboratory where they did experiments on animals.'

'Crikey!' Now she had my attention.

She grinned. 'Actually that's just given me an idea of how to deal with snooty Anne-Marie.'

'Sadie, leave it. She doesn't need dealing with.'

She smirked. 'I think she does.'

My phone started ringing and I saw that it was Dad.

'Hi, Dad. Is everything OK?' I asked, forgetting about Sadie for a moment. Normally Dad phones because he needs to cancel or rearrange something and I was already bracing myself for the disappointment. Then I realised we didn't actually have another day together set up yet.

'Poppy, I'm phoning about Friday. Presumably you're already aware that it's my birthday?' Dad always sounds horribly businesslike on the phone.

'Of course, Dad!' How could he think I'd forget?

'Kristen suggested the three of us go out for an early supper somewhere. She could meet you from school and bring you into town. The two of you can go shopping or something first and then I'll meet you and take you somewhere special for dinner. How's that?'

'Oh.' To say I was surprised would be an understatement. In fact, I loved the idea of going shopping with Kristen, though I knew I'd have to be careful not to sound too enthusiastic in front of Mum.

'Poppy?' He sounded a bit impatient and I realised I hadn't given him an answer.

'That sounds great, Dad.' To actually see Dad on his birthday and get to celebrate it with him would be fantastic! 'I just need to check with Mum.'

'If there's a problem, get her to ring me,' he said (which I knew meant he was prepared to argue with her about it if necessary). 'Otherwise I'll see you on Friday.'

'OK. See you on Friday.'

As I came off the phone I couldn't help wishing we were more like Anne-Marie's family, who always say 'Love you' to each other at the end of every phone call. I think that's really nice, and sometimes I imagine myself saying that to Dad and him saying it back to me. Somehow I can't see that ever happening for real though. Even Mum doesn't do it that often.

'Is everything all right, girls?' Mum asked as she came into the kitchen.

'Yes,' I said quickly. 'Dad just phoned.' I told her what he'd suggested and she said that was fine. 'Mum, when is Lenny coming next?' I asked.

'I'm not sure. She's getting back to me about it. Why?'

'I want to speak to her.'

I saw the wary look Sadie gave me but I didn't care. I went to get changed out of my school uniform.

'So what are you going to tell Lenny?' Sadie demanded, coming into my room without even knocking.

I shrugged. 'Haven't decided yet.'

'You know what, Poppy? I like it here – and I really want to stay. So if you insist on trying to spoil things for me, like telling the social workers about me going to see Alison, then I might just have to speak to them too. Because there's something I know about your mum that I bet they *don't*.'

'What do you mean?'

She came and sat down on my bed uninvited, looking like she was about to confide some big secret. 'I know the *real* reason your mum and my dad fell out.'

'What are you talking about?' I asked impatiently. I wanted to get changed, but I wasn't about to do it in front of her.

'Your mum tried to steal me away from Dad when I

was little. That's why he wouldn't let her see me again. She actually tried to kidnap me!'

'Oh come off it!' I scoffed. 'Mum *loves* children … there's no way she'd ever do anything like that to you or any other child …'

'Dad says she probably thought she was rescuing me, but that she still had no right.' She lowered her voice. 'You see, she wanted to adopt me, and when Dad said no she freaked out, and that's when she tried to kidnap me.' She paused. 'Somehow I don't think she'd be allowed to be a foster carer any longer if social services knew about that, do you?'

I just stared at her in disbelief. I was pretty sure she was making this up, but still …

'You do realise I can easily check this out with Mum?' I said crossly. In fact, this was probably just what I needed to get Mum to see past Sadie's perfect-little-foster-girl act. How would she feel when she heard what Sadie had just said about her, I wondered.

But Sadie was one step ahead of me. 'She won't like me any more if you tell her, which is why you can't tell her. I mean it, Poppy – if you say anything to your mum about this, then the whole deal's off.'

'*What* deal?'

'The deal that *I* won't tell my social worker what your mum did, so long as *you* tell yours that you like me staying here. And you also have to keep quiet about me sneaking off to see Alison.'

I gaped at her. 'Sadie, why are you doing this?'

'I told you. I want to stay here. At least until a better option comes up.'

I stared at her in dismay. Not that I believed any of what she was saying about Mum, but even so …

I couldn't help remembering what Mum had said about falling out with Sadie's dad and wishing she'd handled things differently.

I badly wanted to go and talk to Mum about it but I decided I'd better play it safe and keep quiet for now. Dad was bound to know what had really happened and I was seeing him on Friday. After I'd spoken to him, I could talk to Mum, and she would be forced to see what Sadie was really like.

As for the very minute possibility that Sadie was telling the truth … well, that was so unlikely it wasn't worth thinking about.

And that's when the pain in my tummy started.

I had a sudden flashback to the time just before Mum and Dad split up, when I'd had lots of tummy pains.

Our doctor hadn't found anything physically wrong with me, but had told Mum that tummy aches in children can be a sign of some kind of emotional problem or underlying stress. I curled up on my side on my bed, trying to relax, waiting for the pain to stop. Only it didn't. In fact it started to get worse ...

Chapter Fourteen

At school the next day my first lesson passed slowly. I started getting tummy cramps again soon after I walked into the classroom. I'd taken some painkillers when it had happened the night before and by the time I'd gone to bed I'd felt a lot better.

I hadn't brought any pills with me to school this morning but luckily the pain was easing off by itself by morning break. I had decided to avoid Sadie as much as I could that day, but as I walked into the playground I spotted her chatting to a group of Year Sevens. They were all looking towards the main door, where our headmaster, Mr Jamieson, was standing.

What was Sadie up to now? It was bugging me so much not knowing that in the end I decided to go over and see.

'You're just winding us up,' I heard one of the Year

Seven girls say as I approached them.

As soon as Sadie spotted me she called out, 'Hey, Poppy, I was just pointing out that Mr Jamieson would make a perfect target, the way he stands in one spot like that, at the same place at the same time every morning. He'd be a hitman's dream, don't you think? Even your mum couldn't miss and she's the worst shot in the family!'

'Don't be daft!' I snapped.

'I don't see why he'd be a target for a hitman,' somebody said.

'Ah,' Sadie said, making her voice all mysterious. 'Just because he's our headmaster *now* doesn't mean that's all he *ever* was! We don't know *what* he was doing before he came here, do we?'

'Yeah, cos a lot of gangsters are getting new identities as head teachers these days,' I said.

Sadie hid a grin as Mr Jamieson walked right out into the middle of the playground to tell somebody off. 'Is that a clean shot or what?'

Suddenly there was a loud crack that sounded exactly like a gunshot and I nearly jumped out of my skin. A couple of girls actually screamed. It took a few moments to realise it was only a car backfiring in the teacher's car park, then we all burst out laughing.

'Phew!' Sadie said with a grin when we'd recovered. 'You know, Poppy's mum is always saying that if you can time it right a gunshot can be totally camouflaged by a car backfiring. But my dad says it's always better to use a silencer. Those two are always disagreeing about the best way to do the job, but I guess that's families for you, eh, Poppy?'

'Sadie, stop talking rubbish!' I said. But as I watched the Year Sevens grinning their heads off, clearly hugely entertained if not convinced at all by her story, I could see how much she was enjoying being the centre of attention.

It was only as I walked away from them that I registered something. If she was talking about our 'family business' so openly, that meant she must no longer be trying to hide the fact that I was her cousin.

At lunchtime I headed reluctantly to Mrs Smee's classroom, where she was holding a meeting about the school open afternoon. Apparently Mr Jamieson had decided this week that there wasn't enough already planned, and so he had delegated several more projects to be prepared by certain staff and pupils. Our year, together with Year Nine, had been told to organise a short debate, and Mrs Smee had been put in charge of it. She had told both me and the Year Nine school council rep to round up a few pupils who weren't already contributing to the open day and bring them to a meeting about it at lunchtime today. Mrs Smee had made it very clear that she expected me to be her chief helper on the day since the Year Nine rep had a prior commitment.

The first question Mrs Smee asked when I walked in was whether I was going to take part in the debate myself.

'No way!' I responded, horrified at the thought.

'Well, you may have to if we don't get enough volunteers,' she said tersely. 'And as a member of the school council I shall expect you to pull your weight. I must say that compared with some of the other year reps, you haven't been as visible as you could be, Poppy.' She reached down to scratch her knee under her skirt and I caught a glimpse of the tops of her popsocks.

The first person to arrive at the meeting was Anne-Marie. For as long as I've known her, Anne-Marie's never had a problem speaking out in public, which is why I'd begged her to come today. I'd also begged Josh and Sean, though I wasn't sure they'd turn up.

While we were waiting for more people to arrive I went over to talk to Anne-Marie. 'Sadie found your rhyme,' I warned her. 'Has she said anything to you?'

'Oh, she messaged me this morning,' Anne-Marie said. 'We had quite a long chat. I told her I think it's cool that she's your cousin. She said my poem was pretty funny and that we should totally hang out together since we both love animals. She even says she really wants to come and see my pets. In fact, I might see if she wants to come round after school today. You can come too if you like. You haven't seen our new baby rabbits yet, have you?'

I frowned. Considering Sadie's outburst last night, this just felt all wrong to me. 'Anne-Marie … you're sure Sadie wasn't being sarcastic or pulling your leg or something?'

Anne-Marie scowled at me. 'Why are you asking that? Are you jealous or something?'

'No! It's just …' But I couldn't think how to say what I wanted to say. I wasn't sure what Sadie was up to exactly, but I was certain it wasn't anything good.

'Look … there she is with Josh,' Anne-Marie said, giving me a nudge as the two of them walked in together laughing.

What was Sadie doing here when I hadn't even told her about the meeting? And why was she being so pally with Josh all of a sudden?

'Guess what, Poppy?' Sadie greeted me as if we were the best of friends. 'Me and you are going on a double date this Saturday with Josh and Sean!'

I pulled a face. 'Quit winding me up.'

'She's not. It's not a double date exactly, but we thought we'd all go bowling,' Josh told me with a grin. 'If you and Sean are up for it, that is.'

'Sean should be here any minute,' Sadie said. 'He wasn't planning to come to this but he changed his mind when I told him *you* wanted him to, Poppy.' She gave a knowing little giggle and Josh was smirking too.

I glared at both of them. What was happening here? I felt totally wrong-footed, as if I'd just missed something significant.

Before I could think too much about it Mrs Smee clapped her hands together for silence.

'As you all know,' she began loudly, 'Poppy is this year's Year Eight representative on the school council.'

There was a snigger from the doorway and I saw that Katy and Julia were standing there. I certainly hadn't invited *them*.

'As such,' Mrs Smee continued, 'I have asked her to help me organise a short debate to include as Year Eight and Year Nine's contribution to the open day. So first of all we need a suitable debate topic.'

'How about: *Zoos should be abolished*?' Sadie suggested at once.

Mrs Smee held up her finger for silence. 'If you would please let me finish, Sadie ... I have to say that one topic that always works well is the school uniform argument. Now I wouldn't normally say this, but on this occasion I think we need to choose something tried and tested. Mr Jamieson's rather sudden idea to have this debate has left us with very little time to prepare.'

I wanted to smile as I imagined how Dad would scoff if he could hear her championing a 'tried and tested' debate: 'You should be choosing a current and highly contentious issue, not some nice safe topic that's been discussed to death already!'

'But the ZOOS one will be much better!' Sadie spoke up. 'It won't be too difficult and it's a more important topic. I already know loads of arguments and –'

'Sadie, I want this to be a well researched debate with equal representation for both sides,' Mrs Smee interrupted impatiently. 'I do *not* want it turning into some kind of animal rights presentation!'

Meanwhile, Sean was whispering something to Josh, who seemed to be struggling not to laugh.

Mrs Smee glared at them. 'Perhaps you'd like to share the joke, boys?'

Sean grinned as he readily complied. 'I was just telling Josh something I ... um ... heard about Mr Jamieson. Apparently he's always going on about how Edinburgh Zoo is the best zoo in the UK, because some ancient relative of his actually *founded* it.'

Everyone started talking at once then. Most people thought that would make the zoo debate even more entertaining and that we should definitely do it.

'Though I think Sadie should argue FOR zoos!' Sean said mischievously. 'Just to give herself more of a challenge!'

'I'm NOT arguing for something I don't believe in!' Sadie declared hotly. 'And no way am I going to try and convince people that locking up animals and taking away their freedom is a *good* thing!'

'Yes, yes, calm down ...' Mrs Smee was looking at her watch impatiently. 'I would like six volunteers to make up the two debating teams, please.' She looked at me expectantly and I swiftly ducked my head.

'So are we doing the one about zoos or the one about uniforms?' Anne-Marie asked.

'I'd like volunteers who are prepared to debate *either* topic,' Mrs Smee stated firmly.

Out of the corner of my eye I could see Josh and Sean grinning at each other before raising their hands to volunteer. Anne-Marie volunteered too and so did Sadie. Julia also put her hand up and persuaded Katy to join her. I let out a sigh of relief as Mrs Smee said, 'That's six, then. Good. Now I'm going to quickly hand round these worksheets which have some examples of sensible "for" and "against" arguments. Of course, you can also prepare your own.'

'But these are just arguments for the school uniform debate, Mrs Smee,' Katy said.

'Yes, well, quite frankly I can imagine the zoo debate getting rather one-sided.' She was staring at Sadie as she said that. 'However, if you wish, we can have a debate about zoos at a later point.' She handed round the sheets, completely ignoring everyone's protests.

Sadie looked terribly disappointed and she even stayed behind afterwards to try and convince Mrs Smee to change her mind. I stayed too, but for a different reason. My tummy cramps were back and I felt like I needed to sit down for a minute.

'Are you all right, Poppy?' Mrs Smee asked as she noticed me sitting there clutching my abdomen.

'I've got a bit of tummy pain, that's all,' I muttered.

'Sadie – please take Poppy to the medical room,' she instructed.

'But –' Sadie was scowling.

'It's OK, Mrs Smee … I can go on my own,' I said as I stood up quickly.

Unfortunately Mrs Smee insisted – I had a feeling she was only too pleased to get rid of Sadie herself – and my cousin ended up accompanying me, looking extremely cross.

Chapter Fifteen

'She's a miserable, dictatorial old bat,' Sadie spat out as soon as we were no longer close enough to be heard.

'I think she just wants to play it safe and not offend anyone,' I said quietly.

She snorted. 'Can you imagine what those debates in the House of Commons would be like if nobody wanted to offend anyone else?'

I smiled. Now she was starting to sound like my dad.

She turned to me to say something else, but stopped when she saw me hugging my tummy. 'So what's wrong with you? Is it your time of the month?'

I didn't get what she meant for a moment. 'Huh?'

'You know … is it your *period*?'

'Oh!' To be honest it hadn't even occurred to me that this could be period pain. I hadn't started my periods yet and since Mum had told me she hadn't started hers until she was fourteen, I'd always assumed I had a little while to go.

Sadie was staring at me impatiently. 'Well?'

'I don't think so!' But even as I said it I thought about the low crampy pains I'd been having on and off since last night.

Sadie led me towards the nearest girls' toilets. 'You'd better check. Cos you seem like a big bag of hormones to me.'

'Of *nerves*, you mean,' I mumbled.

'*Hormones*,' she repeated firmly. 'Believe me, I've seen Alison like this enough times to know.'

So I did as she suggested, and once we were safely inside the toilets I went into the nearest cubicle and had a look.

And there it was.

Not bright red blood, but some brownish-red spots. Mum had told me that's how it would probably start.

'Well?' Sadie demanded impatiently from the other side of the door.

'You were right,' I said. I felt a bit stunned actually.

'You've started?'

'I think so.' And I know it probably sounds sappy but I really just wanted to go home and see Mum.

'Told you!' Sadie sounded almost triumphant. 'It's probably why you've been so cranky.' She immediately went all serious and businesslike as she instructed, 'Wait here and I'll go and ask in the office for a sanitary towel or something.'

'No, it's OK!' I called out urgently. 'I've got some stuff in my bag.' As I sorted myself out I could hear Mum's voice in my head telling me I shouldn't be afraid of the changes taking place in my body and that each one was just another step in my journey towards womanhood. I knew she was going to think this was a really special thing and make a massive fuss of me when I got home.

But meanwhile I still had to get through the rest of the day at school.

A few minutes later as I emerged from the cubicle, Sadie looked puzzled as she asked, 'So how come you've got stuff in your bag already?'

'Oh ... Mum put it in there ages ago. She didn't want me to get caught out.'

'Oh.'

I went to the nearest sink to wash my hands, sensing that something was up by the way Sadie had gone so quiet. 'What's wrong?' I asked her.

'Nothing.' But as we left the toilets together she murmured, almost self-consciously, 'You're lucky, that's all.'

'Lucky I've started my periods?' I said, pulling a face, but she was shaking her head emphatically.

'No, no ... not *that*. It's just ... well ... it's just really sweet of your mum to make sure you're all prepared like that.'

Then, of course, I got it. I mean, it must be pretty horrible not having a mum around when you start your periods.

'So have you started yours?' I asked her as casually as I could manage.

She shook her head. 'Alison reckons it won't be long now though,' she added a little defensively.

'Oh, well ... if *Alison* says so ...' Frankly the way Sadie seemed to believe everything this Alison girl told her was starting to bug me a bit.

Sadie looked put out and I realised I'd probably sounded a bit harsh. 'Actually Alison knows a lot,' she said coolly. 'She says I should've got Linda to take me to buy a bra. *As if!*'

I couldn't help looking at her then. She was definitely still a fair way behind me in the bust department – but maybe she wasn't as flat-chested as I'd previously thought.

So far she'd been very private when it came to getting dressed and undressed and she'd always done it in the bathroom or in her bedroom with one of those KEEP OUT signs that hang on the doorknob.

'So why *didn't* you ask Linda?' I said.

'Because it would've been way too embarrassing! Linda is so … well … *not* discreet. I was dreading starting my periods there because I knew she'd make a massive fuss. She was always reminding me that when it happened I wasn't to put any sanitary towels down her loo in case it got blocked! And then, the last time we were in the supermarket she suddenly says in this really loud voice, "You *do* realise tampons can block the toilet too, don't you, hon?"'

I couldn't help laughing. 'At least she called you "hon".'

She rolled her eyes. 'Ha, ha.'

'Mum will take you to get a bra if you want,' I said. 'You should ask her.'

'I don't need her help.'

'OK.' But for once I didn't believe her tough act and I decided that when I got home I'd have a quiet word with Mum about taking Sadie bra shopping.

*

After school Sadie and Anne-Marie were both waiting for me at the gate. That was a first! Then I remembered that Anne-Marie wanted us to go home with her.

Normally I'd have been pleased, but today I felt so achy and tired that I really didn't feel like it. But I didn't want to let Sadie go on her own so I sent Mum a text to let her know we'd be a bit late as we set off for Anne-Marie's to see her baby rabbits.

On the way Anne-Marie chatted away as usual but Sadie was unusually quiet. I just hoped she didn't do or say anything too outrageous when we got there.

Anne-Marie's mum greeted us with a smile, and she was clearly interested to meet Sadie when Anne-Marie introduced her as my cousin.

Then Anne-Marie led us out the back door on to the large covered patio where all the animals are housed in their various hutches and cages. I was looking at Sadie's face as Anne-Marie began to give her a tour. There were two hutches with rabbits inside (including some totally adorable baby ones), a few cages with hamsters and mice, an enclosure with guinea pigs and gerbils and one with some little tortoises.

Sadie was soon having a good look at all of them, her face solemn. As I stroked one of the rabbits I watched her closely. I couldn't shake off the feeling that something was wrong.

'It's like a pet shop,' she murmured – which only made me worry more, since I know she hates pet shops almost as much as she hates zoos. She looked at Anne-Marie in something like amazement. 'I can't believe how many animals you're keeping here.'

'Mum calls it my petting zoo,' Anne-Marie said with a grin.

Sadie flinched. 'I can see why.'

I tensed, half expecting an argument to kick off, but to my amazement it didn't happen. Instead Sadie thanked Anne-Marie for showing her round and started to make for the small gate at the side of the house. 'Can we go out this way or is it locked?'

'Oh, it's never locked. You don't have to go right now, do you? Mum won't mind if you stay a bit longer.'

'I've seen all I want to see, thanks,' Sadie said firmly. 'Come on, Poppy.' And she was already opening the gate and glaring at me to follow her.

Chapter Sixteen

'How are you feeling, Poppy?' Mum asked the next morning as I came into the kitchen, where she and Sadie were already having breakfast. 'Do you want to take some painkillers with you to school?' Just as I'd predicted, she had been making a huge fuss of me. She'd even got a bit teary when I told her my big news. She'd run me a bath after dinner, then sent me to bed with a hot-water bottle and a steaming mug of hot chocolate.

'I think I'll be OK, Mum,' I said.

'Any more bleeding?'

'Just a tiny bit last night. I thought there'd be more.'

'I expect they'll get heavier and more regular with time.'

'Excuse me ... some of us are trying to eat our break-fast here,' Sadie piped up, sounding slightly revolted.

Sadie was getting less and less sympathetic the more Mum doted on me, I'd noticed.

Mum looked across at her sharply, and Sadie must have quickly remembered that she was meant to be sucking up, at least in front of Mum. 'Sorry ... it's just that it's not an *illness*, you know!'

Sadie's mood had been getting progressively worse ever since we'd left Anne-Marie's the day before. On the way home I'd asked her what she'd thought of Anne-Marie's pets and she'd responded by glaring at me and saying that the sight of all those enclosures made her feel sick.

'So why did you say you wanted to see them if you knew it would upset you?' I'd asked impatiently.

But she had told me gruffly that it was none of my business.

Just as I was finishing my cereal the post arrived, and with it a letter for Sadie.

'It's from my dad,' she said a little shakily when Mum gave it to her. She didn't open it in front of us but immediately took it upstairs.

'Mum, can Sadie go and visit her dad in prison if she wants to?' I asked as I sat finishing my toast. It was something I'd been thinking about quite a lot. I couldn't even *imagine* how I'd feel if my mum or dad got sent to prison. I mean, no matter what they'd done, you'd still want to *see* them again, wouldn't you? Unless they'd done something *really* evil.

Mum was nodding. 'Of course she can.'

'So when did she last go?'

'She hasn't been to see him at all yet.'

I frowned. 'Why not?'

'I don't know. She's angry with him, I expect. Hasn't she said anything about it to you?'

I shook my head. 'She doesn't talk about him.'

As I stood up, Mum said, 'Well, be sensitive if she brings it up. She may not have forgiven him yet but he's still her father.'

I nodded, getting myself ready for school before knocking on Sadie's bedroom door. 'It's eight thirty. Are you coming?'

The door was flung open and she stood there in her uniform looking like she'd been crying. Her reddish-brown bob was a lot less sleek and shiny than it usually is and her blue eyes were watery.

'Are you OK?' I asked.

'I'm fine,' she snapped. 'Let's go.'

We walked along our road in silence, with Sadie

seeming moodier than ever. Finally I couldn't stand it any more.

'So is your dad OK?' I asked her.

She looked at me like I was stupid. 'He's locked up in a prison cell. Of course he's not OK.'

I wasn't sure what to say to that so I just nodded dumbly.

After a bit she added, 'He's never been good in confined spaces. The idea of being shut up in prison really frightened him. He got stuck in a lift once and he had a massive panic attack.'

'Oh dear,' I murmured, though inside my head I could also hear Dad's voice saying: 'Well, he should have thought of that before he stole all that money, shouldn't he?'

'I don't suppose his cell … room … whatever they call it … is *that* small,' I said in an awkward attempt to comfort her a little. 'I mean, it's got to be a lot bigger than a lift in any case, cos it's got to have a bed in it and … well … Is it just him in his cell or is he sharing it with somebody else?'

'I don't know!' she snapped. 'He doesn't tell me anything about what it's like there! He just goes on about how sorry he is and how much he wants me to go and see him. And he asks me loads of questions as if he thinks that's going to make me write back.'

'Haven't you, then?' I asked her in surprise. 'Written back, I mean.'

'No.'

'Because you're too angry with him?' I asked hesitantly.

'I'm angry that he thinks he can leave me like that and still get to know what I'm doing every day. I just don't think he has any right, do you?' She paused. 'You know, every time he writes he tells me how the family visiting room isn't scary or anything, and how there's nothing to be afraid of.' She sniffed. 'As if that's the reason I don't go and see him – because I'm scared!'

'Sadie, I know you've every right to be angry with him, but –'

'Well, wouldn't you be angry if *your* dad ditched you like some piece of old rubbish?'

'Sadie, your dad didn't *want* to leave you!' I protested. 'He didn't get sent to prison on purpose!'

'He must have known he might get caught!' she snapped. 'You know he wrote that he only did it for me – so that he could have more money and give me a better life. Who does he think he's kidding? I'll never forgive him for leaving me – for forcing me to go and live with Linda. He's *ruined* my life! That's what he's done! How could he have been so stupid?'

I frowned, realising that she was actually confiding in me more than she ever had before. I was amazed by how much warmer towards her that made me feel.

'But if you hated Linda so much, why didn't you just *tell* your social worker you didn't want to stay with her?' I asked her softly. 'They'd have found you *some* other place to go, wouldn't they?'

'I didn't hate her *then*! OK, so she could be a bit of a pain, but at least it was better than going to live with people I didn't even know! *Then* I found out what she was really like … I'm telling you, *she's* the one who should be put in prison – not my dad!'

'Why? What did she do?' I asked.

'She had all this really gross stuff she'd inherited from her rich old aunt. I nearly threw up the day I first saw it and I told her I wasn't living in the same house as a load of murdered animals, but she just laughed at me and said I was being melodramatic.'

'Sadie, slow down! What are you talking about?' Now I was really confused.

'Her great-aunt's husband was into hunting and she'd inherited all his stuff. She had all these old photos of him with his gun, standing beside some poor animal he'd just killed. It was disgusting. And she had loads of her aunt's old fur coats and jackets and a handbag made of crocodile skin and even an old bearskin rug. The most valuable thing was an antique chess set carved from ivory. Linda said she was going to sell that and I said she should donate the money to this sanctuary for orphaned baby elephants that I'd found for her on the internet, but she said she was keeping the money. Then she said she was going to wear the coats because real fur is back in fashion. I tried to get her to change her mind but she wouldn't listen, so I told Alison and she said the only decent thing to do was to cremate the whole lot on a bonfire. I knew Linda was going out straight from work that Friday, so I arranged to meet Alison and the others after school. I took them back to the house and we cleared out everything she was storing in the spare room and threw it in a pile in the garden. Linda got back before we could set fire to it all though.'

I was stunned. 'Wow,' murmured. 'No wonder she kicked you out.'

Sadie glared at me. 'Whose side are you on?'

'Mine and Mum's! 'You threatened to do the same thing to *us*, remember!'

'Oh yeah,' she admitted, with a sudden grin. 'So I did. Only it turns out you don't have any fur coats or bearskin rugs or ivory chessboards. Luckily for you ...'

I gaped at her as she put her earbuds in and walked the rest of the way to school without speaking to me. Though she did stay close enough to grab half of the space under my umbrella when it started to rain.

Chapter Seventeen

It seemed to rain more or less non-stop for the rest of the week.

At morning breaktime on Friday it was still wet so I headed straight for the canteen. I was really looking forward to going out with Dad and Kristen that evening and I had the *Just William* book wrapped up in posh paper inside my schoolbag. (Don't ask me how long I searched for the perfect wrapping paper because I'm not going to tell you!)

I was feeling happier than I had in a while. With the threat to our house no longer present, all I needed to do was prove that Sadie's accusation about Mum was a lie and there would be nothing left for Sadie to blackmail me with.

The only thing spoiling my happiness (other than the rubbish weather) was that our visit to Amy in her new home the following day had just been postponed because Amy had chickenpox.

I told Anne-Marie about it as I caught up with her outside the canteen. 'You know, I feel really bad that Amy has chickenpox and we aren't there to look after her,' I said gloomily.

'Her new mum and dad will look after her,' Anne-Marie said (which was exactly what Mum had said as well).

'I guess,' I grunted, though I still wasn't convinced that anybody could do as good a job as Mum and me at cheering up a sick preschooler.

'So when will you get to see her?'

'Next Saturday, hopefully, if she's better. Look, there's a table … let's grab it.'

There was a really big queue for the tuck shop and the room was full of people escaping the rain.

'So how's it going with Sadie?' Anne-Marie asked as we sat down.

'OK, I suppose. It's better, but she's different every time I talk to her. And Mum still seems to be on her side all the time.' Lenny was coming round with Sadie's social worker at four o'clock that afternoon, and at first I'd been afraid Mum would want me to be there and that I wouldn't be allowed to go out with Kristen after school.

But in fact Mum was so cool about it that I started to wonder if she'd arranged the social work visit today on purpose, grateful that I wouldn't be there to put my foot in it.

'Maybe it'll get better the more you get to know her. Do you know where she gets her hair cut, by the way? I think it looks really cool.' After I replied that I didn't know, Anne-Marie pulled a magazine from her bag. 'Look. I found this great quiz that you can use to work out your face shape. It gives you tips on the best way to put on make-up and your most flattering hairstyle and stuff.'

'Let's see.' I have to admit I love doing these sorts of quizzes.

'I'm heart shaped!' she added with a smirk.

'Trust you,' I said. 'OK, let's do mine.' I started to read the instructions. First you had to look through some diagrams and tick the ones you thought looked most like you. 'This is a bit difficult if you don't have a mirror,' I complained.

'Ta-da!' Anne-Marie produced a small mirror from her bag and gave it to me. 'Wait.' She grabbed my hair and pulled it back off my face as if she was putting it in a ponytail. 'Now look.'

'What are you two doing?' Sadie arrived at our table and sat down without being invited.

'It's just a quiz to work out your face shape,' Anne-Marie said. 'You can have a go after Poppy if you like.' She'd been a lot more friendly towards Sadie ever since Sadie had shown such an interest in her animals, though I still had an uncomfortable feeling about that.

'I've done one of those before,' Sadie said, sounding a bit dismissive. 'Anyway, you can see just by *looking* at your face what shape it is. Mine's oval. Poppy's going to be rectangular – or maybe even square.'

'Shut up,' I snapped at her. But by the end of the questionnaire, when I had scored 'Mostly B's', I realised she was right.

'Told you so,' Sadie said with a smirk.

'No way do I have a square face!' I protested.

'You know, you actually *do*,' Anne-Marie added seriously. 'Your jawline is definitely angular … isn't it, Sadie?'

'Definitely,' Sadie said with a grin. She pointed to the diagram of the most obviously square face, which was far and away the least attractive of all the faces on the page. 'I'd say that's the closest.'

Anne-Marie tactfully flipped the page over. 'Look at this, Poppy!'

There was a whole section on glasses.

'Let me see!' Sadie made a grab for the magazine. 'So what type do they say go best on a square face?'

'Oval or round,' Anne-Marie said, grabbing it back.

'There you go!' Sadie sat back, looking at me triumphantly. 'That explains why your glasses look so *wrong* on you, Poppy.'

'It says here that rectangular glasses like yours are best suited to round or oval faces,' Anne-Marie added gravely. 'Too bad your mum won't let you get new ones, Poppy.'

'Hey, maybe you could alter your face shape instead,' Sadie said.

'Oh yes!' Anne-Marie joined in. 'My mum is always complaining that whenever she goes on a diet she loses loads of weight from her face before she loses it from anywhere else.'

'Losing fat won't help,' Sadie said. 'It's her bone structure that's the issue and there's no changing that. Well … not without a chisel!' She giggled.

To my horror I found myself feeling a bit wobbly inside, like I might be going to cry. I know this is going to sound pathetic but I'd honestly thought I had a pretty nice face up until that moment. Mum has always praised my high cheekbones and I've always been happy enough with how I look in photographs. Usually Mum comments on how photogenic I am. But I guess everyone must have just been keeping quiet about the squareness.

'It doesn't really matter about your glasses since you don't need to wear them outside of class,' Anne-Marie was saying in a consoling voice. I think she had just realised that I wasn't finding this at all funny. 'Let's see what hairstyle you should have instead. Oh, look, Poppy! That's just like yours already.'

'Except her hair should be longer to divert attention away from her jawline,' Sadie pointed out.

And at that point I had had enough. Anne-Marie started to say something else, but I was already standing up and glaring at both of them through alarmingly blurry vision that had nothing to do with my short-sightedness. 'I'm off! I'll leave you two to admire your perfectly shaped faces together, shall I?'

'Poppy, don't be daft –' Anne-Marie began, but I was already turning my back on them and stalking off as the first tears began to fall. There was no way I was going to let them see how stupidly upset I was.

Maths was our next lesson that morning. Miss Benkowski had written some questions up on the whiteboard so I had to wear my glasses. I immediately felt self-conscious.

I soon noticed Julia and Katy, who sit at the next table, giving me amused looks. I felt myself flushing as I resisted the urge to take off my glasses before I'd even read the first question.

I turned round to look at Sadie, who was seated two rows behind. Her head was down and it seemed to me that she was avoiding catching my eye.

'Poppy – unless you've got eyes in the back of your head, I'm not sure that's such a good position from which to view the board,' Miss Benkowski remarked lightly.

I turned back to face the front, self-consciously removing my glasses. Now I couldn't read anything on the whiteboard but at least I wasn't looking quite so hideous.

As the school day drew to a close I began to forget about my face as I looked forward to my evening with Dad and Kristen. The fact that Kristen was meeting me from school and taking me shopping first was an added bonus – not that I'd ever admit that to Mum. It's not that going shopping with Mum isn't enjoyable. It's just that Mum always tends to go for shoes and clothes that are sensible and comfortable rather than fashionable. The only exception is if we find something for a good price in a second-hand shop. Which I guess is another reason why I like shopping in charity shops so much!

Anne-Marie tried to make up with me a couple of times that afternoon but I kept ignoring her. Josh mentioned the bowling idea again, but I told him there was no way I was going anywhere with Sadie this weekend. So we agreed to postpone the bowling to another time. On my way out of school I pretended not to hear her when Sadie called out to me. Instead I whizzed out through the school gates and off along the road where Kristen had texted that she was waiting for me.

I spotted her straight away, leaning on the bonnet of her cream-coloured Mini. Her blonde hair was loose and half pushed back under a red beret. 'Hello, Poppy,' she greeted me cheerfully. 'How was school?'

'OK,' I muttered, suddenly feeling shy.

She looked a little bit awkward too as she opened the door and invited me to get in.

'Nice car,' I mumbled.

'Thanks.' She smiled at me as she was pulling on her seat belt. 'We're meeting your dad at six o'clock at the Italian restaurant on the high street. It's up to you what we do until then. Would you like to go and have a look round the shops maybe? Or I could take you somewhere for a drink and a cake if you're hungry?'

As she pulled out of the parking space I noticed that Kristen wasn't asking me to twist round to look and see if any cars were coming. Mum is always doing that and I hate it because it makes me feel like it's *my* responsibility to ensure nothing crashes into us.

I don't know what possessed me to say the next thing. 'Actually, Kristen, I really need some new glasses. Can I borrow some money to get them and I'll ask Dad to pay you back?'

'Oh, but don't you want to choose them with your mum?'

'She hasn't got time and I'm really struggling at school with the ones I've got.'

'Oh dear.' She looked concerned.

'Oh, I don't mean struggling to see properly,' I quickly reassured her. 'They're the right strength and everything. I mean struggling to cope with how dorky I look in them.'

'I see!' She laughed, and after that we started chatting away pretty easily. She told me she knew how I felt because she'd had to wear glasses as a kid and in those days they didn't have all the nice frames they have now.

'So are you wearing contacts?' I asked, staring at her

perfect green eyes while trying to work out what shape her face was.

'Oh yes. I couldn't survive without them.'

'I want them as soon as I'm allowed,' I said. 'But knowing Mum, that won't be until I leave home.'

She smiled but didn't join in with my gentle dig at Mum. I realised this was the first one of Dad's girlfriends I'd ever joked with even a tiny bit about my mother.

We parked in the multistorey car park, where Kristen reversed into a space with the aid of her parking sensors. 'I wish our car had those,' I told her. 'Mum hates reverse parking and she's always making me get out of the car to check she doesn't bump into stuff. Only then she just gets in a flap about bumping into *me*!'

Kristen smiled, saying carefully, 'Well, I expect you're rather precious to her.'

We went straight to the optician's Kristen told me she uses herself, where they insisted on testing my eyes to confirm my prescription before showing us their range of frames. I spent ages choosing, and since I knew Dad would be paying I didn't bother about the price. I told Kristen I had to get round or oval frames for my face shape and she didn't tell me not to be silly (as I'm sure Mum would have done). When I'd chosen the frames

Kristen phoned Dad to check it was OK for her to buy them for me. She came off the phone with a smile after he told her to go ahead. I smiled too. I'd half expected him to cross-examine me about my reason for needing new ones before agreeing to anything.

After we left the optician's – they'd told us the glasses should be ready for collection the next week – Kristen took me to help her choose a birthday cake for Dad. She had a packet of candles in her bag and she said she was going to hide the cake from Dad and get the restaurant to bring it out with the coffee. I'd never seen Dad blowing out birthday candles. It just seemed too childish a thing to expect him to do somehow. But Kristen clearly didn't agree because she chose a red sports car birthday cake and said we would come back and pick it up before the shop closed.

The high street is pedestrianised and there are quite a few charity shops. 'Have you ever tried to go into a charity shop with my dad?' I asked Kristen out of curiosity.

Kristen pulled a face as she answered, 'Actually I prefer to leave him behind when I go into *any* kind of shop! I like to take my time and he gets rather impatient.'

'He goes in and out of the shops really quickly, doesn't he?' I said. 'Mum says he hates the fact that women *browse*.'

She laughed. 'Sounds about right.'

'I never used to like browsing either, but now he says I'm worse than Mum.'

She laughed again. 'In that case I'm sure you and I are perfectly matched.'

It was fun looking round the shops with her – kind of like being with a really cool older sister. For the briefest moment I thought that maybe living with Dad wouldn't be so bad after all, so long as Kristen was around.

'Kristen, how old are you?' I asked her, suddenly wondering about the age gap between her and Dad.

'Forty-two.'

'Really?' I'd honestly thought she was younger than that. I mean, that was only a couple of years younger than Mum, but Mum didn't seem nearly as youthful, either in appearance or attitude. 'You know, you're not like Dad's usual girlfriends.'

'How's that, then?'

'I don't really know. You're just different.' I paused. 'In a good way, I mean.'

She smiled. 'Well, so long as it's in a good way.'

And Dad's different when he's with you, I thought. *Definitely in a good way*. In fact, I didn't think I'd ever seen Dad this happy and relaxed with a girlfriend before.

Chapter Eighteen

Dad was half an hour late for dinner, but Kristen and I agreed that because it was his birthday we wouldn't make a fuss. We'd eaten the whole bread basket by the time he arrived – something Mum never lets me do because she says it'll ruin my appetite for my meal.

I have to say that once Dad had had a few sips of wine ~~and~~ opened Kristen's present – which was a pair of really beautiful cufflinks – he seemed to relax. In any case he gave Kristen a thank-you kiss right on the lips – just a peck, but it was still a bit embarrassing.

That's when I plucked up the courage to give him the book which I'd wrapped up so perfectly and been carrying around in my schoolbag all day. I held my breath as I waited for his reaction as he opened it.

'What beautiful paper. Don't rip it, Peter,' Kristen

u can't

153

said, and if I had been able to drag my eyes away from Dad, I'd have smiled at her gratefully.

'*Just William*!' Dad exclaimed with a laugh as he held it up to show her, and for a moment I thought he might think it was just a token jokey sort of gift rather than his actual proper present. But then he said, 'Where on earth did you find this?' as if he realised it hadn't been that easy to locate.

'That second-hand bookshop near the park,' I told him. 'Do you like it? It's not a first edition or anything but it's very old and it's got some really nice illustrations inside.'

'It's perfect – and very thoughtful,' he responded, leaning across to give me a kiss on the cheek before laying the book to one side. I wouldn't have minded if he'd sat there flicking through it for a while but I guess you have everything. I reminded myself that Dad thinks it's bad manners to read at the table and that he'd probably have a closer look at it later.

'So you and Kristen have been having a nice time then, have you, Poppy?' Dad said with a smile.

I nodded. 'Thanks for the glasses, Dad.' And I reminded him how much money he owed Kristen.

They both laughed for some reason and Dad assured

me that he would definitely reimburse her and that he'd try and pick them up for me next week.

The rest of the meal passed by cheerfully until Kristen asked me how I liked being a school councillor and I realised Dad must have told her about it. I wondered if he'd also told her how much persuasion I'd needed to apply for the job in the first place.

'Actually it's turning out to be a real hassle,' I answered truthfully. 'And now I've got to help organise a debate for our open day.'

'Really?' Dad's ears pricked up immediately. 'I could give you a few pointers if you like. I used to be head of our school debating team when I was in the sixth form.'

Of course you were, I thought with a sigh.

Kristen just smiled. She'd probably been head of her school debating team too, I thought. Unlike poor Mum, who'd told me she'd been struck dumb with nerves at school every time she'd had to speak in front of even a tiny audience.

'So I hope you're taking part in this debate, Poppy?' Dad said. 'It will be an excellent opportunity to get in some public speaking experience.'

'I'm chairing it,' I mumbled. Mrs Smee had insisted and I hadn't managed to wriggle out of it.

'Excellent! When is it? I'll see if I can come.'

I was momentarily taken by surprise. 'Well, it's two weeks today, but it's in the afternoon. You'll be at work, won't you?'

'If I'm not in court, I'll take the time off.'

'Oh.' I didn't know what else to say. I couldn't deny that I was flattered he wanted to be there. But I was also terrified. It would be bad enough messing up in front of Mum and all my friends. But messing up with Dad looking on …

The birthday cake Kristen had chosen went down much better than I'd thought it would. Dad did look a bit embarrassed when the waiter brought it out, and he clearly found us singing 'Happy Birthday' to him a lot less jolly than we did. But he kept a smile on his face and he ate the cake even though I know he hates all that sugary icing.

'Next year you'll have to blow out *fifty* candles,' I teased him. And I found myself hoping Kristen would be around to buy him a cake then as well. Or maybe even bake him one, which would be better still. (I'd have to drop a few hints to her about that.)

At the end of the meal Dad said he would take me home and Kristen said goodbye to me and went off to get her own car. She and Dad were meeting back at his place afterwards, and I couldn't help wondering if she'd be staying the night.

Dad had helped Kristen on with her jacket and now he did the same with my blazer. Dad is a real gentleman that way – helping ladies on with their coats and opening doors for them and all that stuff. In fact, if Mum ever tells me that's another thing she used to like about Dad but now finds irritating, then I'm going to contradict her because it certainly makes me feel special when he does it for me.

As we walked back to his car he asked if I'd enjoyed my evening. I nodded that I had and he said, 'You seem to be getting on well with Kristen.'

I nodded again, smiling as I told him, 'Well, she's nice and normal – not like your other girlfriends.'

He gave me a sideways look. 'Is it my imagination or have you been getting cheekier recently?'

I just kept grinning. '*And* she puts you in a good mood.'

'Are you implying that I'm not *always* in a good mood?'

'Actually – *yes!*'

At which point he started to laugh.

Once we were in the car we both got more serious.

'So how are things going with Sadie?' he asked me.

'Oh, OK, I guess,' I murmured, avoiding looking at him.

Dad was giving me a searching look. 'Are you sure?'

I know he doesn't like it when he thinks I'm keeping stuff from him, and I wanted to tell him the truth. But at the same time I knew I had to be careful if I was going to complain to him about Sadie. If he thought I was seriously unhappy he would definitely intervene, and there was no way I wanted to start up another big row between him and Mum.

'Your mother should have asked you before agreeing to take her in,' Dad muttered.

'Well, she *is* Mum's niece,' I said in as neutral a voice as I could manage. 'I guess Mum feels like it's her duty to help her.' I paused uncertainly. This was my chance to ask him about that crazy accusation Sadie had made. 'Actually, Sadie told me something about Mum and I'm sure it can't be true ... something she says Mum did when we were little ...'

'What?' Dad prompted me.

'She says Mum wanted to adopt her and that she tried to kidnap her when Sadie's dad said no. That's not true, is it?'

'Of course not!' Dad was shaking his head dismissively.

'Though I can imagine Kevin seeing it that way and possibly even telling Sadie that story. Your mother was looking after Sadie a lot, you see, while Kevin worked, and she got very attached to her. She didn't think Kevin was coping very well as a single parent, plus he's definitely always been a bit of a shifty character, so she offered for Sadie to move in with us, at least for a while. Well ... Kevin was horrified. I advised your mother to drop it but she wouldn't, and they ended up having a terrible row. Kevin got quite paranoid about the whole thing. He seemed to think we might be plotting to take him to court to get Sadie away from him. He not only made new childcare arrangements, he stopped us from seeing Sadie altogether. Your mother was heartbroken, as you can imagine. Sadie was like a second daughter to her by then. We actually *did* consider trying to take the matter to court at that point, just in order to get *some* ongoing contact with Sadie, but in the end we decided that we probably wouldn't get anywhere and that fighting over her like that wouldn't be in her best interests.'

'That's awful!' I exclaimed, because I hadn't known any of this until now. 'But it doesn't sound like Mum did anything *wrong.*'

'Well, no ... though I dare say she could have been a

lot more tactful with the way she approached Kevin instead of letting her emotions rule as usual.'

'Yes, but nothing so wrong that social services would think she was unsuitable as a foster carer.'

Dad gave me a sharp look. 'What exactly has Sadie been saying to you?'

I bowed my head, hiding my face as I mumbled, 'Nothing.'

'Poppy, don't lie to me.'

I started to squirm, then stopped myself. After all, I wasn't in the witness box and Dad didn't have his wig on, even if he *was* using his courtroom voice.

'Dad, I'm not under oath here,' I said in as reasonable a tone as I could manage. 'Just because I don't want to tell you something doesn't make it ... I don't know ... contempt of court or something like that.'

His eyebrows shot up in surprise, but he recovered pretty quickly. 'I wasn't implying otherwise, Poppy! I don't like you lying to me because, quite simply, it prevents me from helping you.'

'I know that, Dad,' I said. And as kindly as possible I added, 'It's just that sometimes it's better if I sort stuff out on my own.'

Chapter Nineteen

As I unlocked our front door and waved goodbye to Dad, who had been watching me from the car, I heard music coming from the kitchen. It wasn't all that late but I felt really tired.

I'd been thinking non-stop since Dad had told me what had actually happened. Because even though Sadie's story about Mum wasn't true, I couldn't just forget about it. Not now that I knew how close I had come to having Sadie in my life all along.

Mum and Sadie were sitting at the kitchen table talking. The radio was on and they were flicking through Mum's photo album. They had their backs to me and when they didn't turn round I realised they hadn't heard me come in. Mum was showing Sadie some baby photographs and I decided not to interrupt them. But I couldn't resist standing outside the door to listen.

'You do know your mother was only twenty-two when you were born?' Mum was telling Sadie. 'I was ten years older so I tried to help her as much as I could, but she always argued with me about every little thing.'

'Dad says she argued a lot with him too,' Sadie said.

Mum sighed. 'That sounds like Kim.'

'Dad says that he always loved me more than she did. Is *that* true, do you think?'

'I don't know about that, Sadie, but I do know Kim just didn't seem cut out to be a mother. She always put her own needs first.'

'Dad says she wrote you a letter after she left,' Sadie murmured. 'She never wrote one to me.'

'It was a very short letter. All it said was that she'd changed her name and we should think of her as dead from now on because she wasn't coming back.' Mum paused. 'I don't know about your dad, but that's certainly what I've been trying to do since then – think of her as dead and gone. It's the only way I've found to move on.'

'I keep thinking that one day she might contact me,' Sadie murmured in such a quiet voice I could hardly hear her.

'Just don't get your hopes up too much,' Mum said gently. 'I knew Kim for longer than anyone and I'd honestly be surprised if she ever did. And even then I don't think you could trust her not to take off again whenever she got the urge.' Mum paused, presumably to show her another photo, because a few moments later she said, 'That's Kim when she was fifteen. My parents had her very late so at that point Mum was nearly sixty and Dad in his seventies, and Dad's health was never good after his stroke, poor thing. Kim was always running off and being brought back again. Sometimes she'd be gone for days, occasionally for a week or more. Our mother was always worried sick about her.' Mum paused again. 'You know, sometimes I think Kim did the best thing for you that she could, making a clean break and leaving once and for all. Better than coming in and out of your life all the time, making you love her, then leaving again.'

Sadie made a funny choking sound and I realised she had started to cry.

'Oh, Sadie, I'm sorry,' Mum murmured. She was probably hugging Sadie, though I couldn't see.

Silently I tiptoed back to the front door. I didn't want them to know I'd overheard their conversation. I was going to have to pretend I'd just this second arrived home.

I gave them a few more minutes, then I opened the front door and slammed it shut this time. I called out 'HI!' before treading loudly across the hall.

I took as long as possible hanging up my jacket, and by the time I reached the kitchen they had closed the photo album. Sadie was rubbing her eyes and Mum was on her feet filling the kettle.

'Hi,' all three of us blurted out awkwardly at more or less the same time.

'How was dinner?' Mum asked me.

'Fine,' I answered quickly. 'We went to that really nice Italian restaurant ... I had ravioli and a cream horn.' I paused. 'How about you? How was your meeting with Lenny?'

'Fine.' Mum was reaching into the cupboard for the teabags. 'They're coming back next week to speak to you as well. I've tried to tell them you need more time to adjust but they're getting very anxious to know how *you* feel about Sadie staying with us more permanently.'

I saw that Sadie was looking at me intently. She must think she still had the same hold over me as before.

'OK,' I said. 'Next time they come I'll tell them.' And I turned round and went upstairs, feeling Mum and Sadie both staring after me.

That weekend passed quickly, even though nothing much happened. When Sadie cornered me to ask exactly *what* I intended to tell our social workers, I let her think I was still buying into her kidnapping story and that I would therefore say whatever she wanted. It was tempting to tell her the truth, but the last thing I wanted was Sadie inventing some new threat to try and keep me quiet.

I couldn't deny that I found Sadie a lot less terrifying now that I'd got to know her better, but the main thing that still worried me was how readily (and convincingly) she was prepared to lie to get what she wanted. And Mum just couldn't seem to see that. In fact, my mother still seemed totally sucked in by Sadie's whole prodigal daughter routine – or prodigal *niece*, if there was such a thing.

I woke up feeling tired and grumpy on Monday morning. I wished I could skip school and stay in bed. Instead I staggered into the bathroom and I was just splashing cold water on my face to wake myself up when I heard a beep and looked up to see Sadie's phone lying on the bathroom shelf. A new text had just come in. It was from Alison:

Be careful on Saturday. Don't get caught. Overnight coach booked for Sunday night. Be at bus station 10pm.

'Let me in! I need to get something!' Sadie was thumping impatiently on the door.

'Hold your horses! I'll be out in a minute!' I shouted back. I decided it was probably best to pretend I hadn't seen her text, though I badly wanted to know what was going on. What was happening on Saturday? And why was Alison texting her about an overnight coach?

Maybe I should tell Mum. But then again there was a part of me that thought that whatever Sadie was planning, I should just wait and see how it all played out.

I got dressed and ate my breakfast as quickly as I could, and I managed to leave the house ahead of Sadie. I wanted to tell Josh about that text and see what *he* thought about it. Josh is always really sensible about this kind of thing.

'Poppy, wait!' I had nearly reached school when I heard Sadie behind me, running to catch up.

'POPPY!' Josh was calling to me from up ahead, his schoolbag swinging beside him. I ignored Sadie and kept walking towards Josh. 'Sean and I went bowling with Leo at the weekend,' he said as I reached him. 'It was great! You have to come with us this Saturday, OK?'

'I'm seeing Amy this Saturday.'

'Oh yeah, I forgot. A week on Saturday, then?'

'Can Sean make that one?'

He grinned. 'Oh, don't you worry – we'll check *he* can make it before we book anything!'

'I wasn't worrying, I was just asking,' I said stroppily. 'Listen, I've been thinking … maybe we should ask Anne-Marie if she wants to come.'

'Why?' He didn't sound keen.

'Well, it's a bit mean to leave her out and I don't think she does much on a Saturday.'

I'd also been thinking that if we didn't ask her, and Sadie and I went with the boys, then it might seem a bit like a double date, which would be embarrassing.

'Anne-Marie is going to be at her aunt and uncle's all day this Saturday,' Sadie said, having caught us up and overheard the last part of our conversation.

'Poppy can't make this –' Josh began, but I cut him off.

'How do you know that?' I demanded sharply.

Sadie shrugged. 'I asked her what she was doing at the weekend and she told me.'

'So are *you* free this Saturday?' I asked her. 'Or do *you* have something on too?'

She gave me a guarded look. 'Like what?'

I shrugged. 'I don't know. Anything. You tell me.'

'Look – there's Sean,' Josh exclaimed, pointing at a very small figure in the distance. 'He'd better hurry or he's going to be late again and then he's really gonna be in trouble! Leo's threatened to make him ride to school with him if he's late for registration one more time.'

We could hear the school bell ringing and in the distance we saw Sean break into a run, but he was too far away for us to wait for him. The three of us carried on into school, and after Josh had gone off with some other Year Nines, Sadie and I headed for our registration room.

Anne-Marie joined us just as we were having a discussion about Sean.

'He's a total wuss if you ask me,' Sadie was saying dismissively. 'Letting himself be bossed around all the time by someone who isn't even his proper dad!'

'He's *not* a wuss,' I protested hotly. 'He just doesn't want to get on Mr Anderson's bad side. Plus if he gets grounded then he won't be able to come bowling with us, will he?'

'He could if he had any guts. He doesn't *have* to do what his bossy stepdad says. I think it's pathetic the way he acts around him – like he really looks up to him and wants to please him all the time or something.'

'Even if he does, what's it to you?' I said. 'Anyway, it's probably really *nice* for Sean to finally have a dad after so long.'

'Poppy's right,' Anne-Marie agreed. 'You know his dad died when he and his sister were little, don't you? I just think that's *so* sad.'

Sadie's eyes narrowed as she gave Anne-Marie a cold look. 'It's not *that* sad.'

Anne-Marie opened her mouth to speak, then shut it again.

'*What?*' Sadie demanded defiantly as she saw the looks we were both giving her. 'People die all the time. It's not that big a deal.'

'That's really mean, Sadie,' I said with feeling.

'Oh, stop being so pathetic!' she snapped before storming off.

'I can't believe she said that!' Anne-Marie said as we watched her go. 'I mean, what was all that about?'

I shrugged like I didn't know, but in actual fact I had a pretty good idea. And I vowed to steer well clear of the subject of fathers with Sadie from now on.

Chapter Twenty

'So what do you think I should do?' I asked Josh at lunchtime as the two of us headed for the far side of the
playground to sit on the wall. I had told him about the
text I'd accidently seen and we were speculating about
what it meant.

'If you weren't going to see Amy, you could follow her
on Saturday and see where she goes,' he said.

'See where *who* goes?' Sean asked as he joined us.

Before I could stop him Josh had told Sean about the
text.

'Sounds like she's planning to do something dodgy on
Saturday and then leave town on Sunday!' Sean joked.
'Why don't you just ask her? She left her phone in the
bathroom and you saw her text. What's the big deal?'

'Uh-oh, here she comes,' Josh said as he spotted Sadie
walking across the playground.

'Just leave this to me,' Sean said. 'I'll soon get the information out of her.'

'Sean, just leave it –' I began but he ignored me and greeted Sadie the second she was in earshot.

'Hi, Sadie! We were just talking about you!'

'Really?' She didn't look impressed.

'Yeah, we were talking about bowling this Saturday. I know Poppy can't come, but what about you?'

She looked a bit surprised. 'I guess I could come in the morning.'

'Oh yeah? So what have you got planned in the afternoon, then?'

She scowled. 'None of your business.'

'Come on, Sadie. It can't be that big a secret. Not unless you're going to rob a bank or … I don't know … spring your dad from prison or something.'

Sadie went pale at the mention of her dad.

I immediately looked sharply at Josh. He'd promised not to tell anyone about Sadie's dad being in prison.

'Hey, *I* never mentioned it,' Josh hissed, frowning at my accusing look.

Sadie looked fit to explode. 'How do you know about my dad?' she asked Sean furiously.

'Oh, well …' He looked wide-eyed. 'I only know cos I overheard Leo, but –'

'WHAT?' Sadie didn't let him finish before she jumped up. 'Mr Jamieson said the teachers would keep it confidential. And now your stepdad is spreading it round the school?'

'No, of course not! No one else knows except me!'

'He wasn't meant to tell *anyone*! That's it! I'M GOING TO REPORT HIM RIGHT NOW!' She turned to leave.

'What? No! It wasn't like that, Sadie –' Sean reached out to stop her going, and the second his hand made contact with her shoulder she whirled round and whacked him hard in the face.

'SADIE!' I screamed as she ran off towards the school building.

Sean fell backwards against the railings, blood spurting from his nose. Josh and I rushed over to him.

Sean's hands were covering his face but the blood was trickling through his fingers. 'We have to stop her telling,' he cried out in a bunged-up voice.

'Sean, your nose is bleeding! Sit down and tip your head forward,' I told him, pulling tissues out of my bag at a rate of knots. Thankfully I knew what to do because Amy used to get nosebleeds sometimes.

'I have to go after her,' Sean repeated desperately.

'Josh, *you go*!' I told him. 'Sean, just stay here and squeeze the top of your nose.'

Josh rushed off and Sean stopped trying to stay on his feet and sat down on the wall instead. Fortunately nobody else seemed to have noticed what had happened. The last thing Sean needed right now was an audience.

Thankfully his nosebleed didn't take long to stop. 'I don't *think* it's broken … it's not bent or anything,' I told him as I peered closely at his nose.

'It hurts,' he grunted. 'And I need to change this shirt before anyone sees.' His shirt was splattered with blood. 'Oh God, if Leo hears about this he's going to be really mad!'

'Let's just wait here for a minute. Maybe Josh managed to stop Sadie telling.'

We sat together on the wall in silence for a couple of minutes.

'So when did Leo … Mr Anderson … tell you about Sadie's dad?' I asked him awkwardly.

He looked uncomfortable. 'He didn't *tell* me! It's just … I overheard him talking to Mum about it one night. It was really late and I'd gone downstairs for some water. I know I shouldn't have been listening in. I never even told them I'd overheard.' He sighed. 'Now I've gone and landed Leo in it!' His voice had actually risen up a pitch at the thought of Leo getting into trouble because of what he'd done.

'You never know – Josh might have stopped her telling by now,' I said. 'Come on. Let's go and find out.'

He reached up to touch his nose self-consciously as we walked across the playground. 'Does it look really bad?'

'It's pretty red. You're probably going to get a big bruise.'

'Good,' he said matter-of-factly. 'The bigger the better. I need it to look as bad as possible so Leo and Mum feel sorry for me. Otherwise they're going to kill me.'

'Oh, Sean.' I couldn't help grinning despite the situation. 'Look, there's Josh,' I said as we stepped inside the school building. Our head teacher's room is on the ground floor and Josh was walking away from it, towards us. He was alone and he looked worried.

'Where's Sadie?' I asked at once.

'I couldn't stop her,' he said gloomily. 'She told Mr Jamieson's secretary she needed to speak to him urgently. She's in his office right now, reporting Mr Anderson for breach of confidentiality.'

*

174

Once Mr Jamieson got involved everything happened really fast.

Josh and Sean and I all got interviewed very briefly in his office. Mr Jamieson said he wanted 'corroboration of the facts' before he took any further action. We told him how Sadie had punched Sean and given him a nosebleed. I felt no loyalty towards my cousin now that she had just made a heap of trouble for everyone.

Mum was called and asked to come up to the school immediately. I was told to take Sean to the medical room to get checked over by our school nurse. Sadie was taken off by the school counsellor Mrs Thomson to talk to her until Mum got here, and Josh was sent back to class.

Up in the medical room, as soon as the nurse had finished checking Sean and writing her report, she left us alone. Sean immediately started panicking that Leo might lose his job or face some kind of disciplinary hearing or something.

'Oh, Sean, I'm sure it won't come to that,' I tried to reassure him.

'Why couldn't I just keep my big mouth shut?' he mumbled, holding his head in his hands. '*Ouch!*' Clearly he'd forgotten about his nose.

'Anyway, Sadie's got to be in more trouble than you,'

I said, trying to make him feel better. 'She actually punched you. She'll probably get suspended.'

Just then the door of the medical room opened and Mr Anderson came in. He looked worried and he frowned even more when he saw Sean. I can't say I blamed him. The bruising was coming out pretty badly around Sean's nose now.

'I heard what happened. Are you OK?' Mr Anderson squatted down in front of him, peering closely at his face and ignoring his protests as he lightly felt the bridge of his nose. 'Looks like she packed quite a punch. I don't think you'll be living this one down in a hurry, mate.' He turned to me. 'Poppy, your mother's just arrived. Mr Jamieson wants you to wait outside his office in case he needs to speak to you again.'

'You heard *why* she punched me, right?' Sean whispered, sounding nervous.

'Oh yes, I heard, all right,' Mr Anderson replied. 'Mr Jamieson just hauled me into his office to inform me.'

Sean gulped. 'Leo, I'm really sorry.'

'Yes, well, we need to talk. But first we need to get your face checked out. Come on. I'm dropping you off at home. Your mother's phoning the doctor to see if you can get an appointment this afternoon.'

'What about you, Leo?' Sean asked anxiously. 'Did I get *you* in a lot of trouble?'

'We'll talk about it at home.'

And not for the first time I felt a rush of warmth towards Sean, because it was so obvious how much he cared. Unlike Sadie. I sighed. Why did she have to be such a troublemaker? And why did she have to be my cousin?

After ten minutes of sitting outside Mr Jamieson's office on my own I was called in. Either Mum or Mr Jamieson or both seemed to be under the mistaken impression that when it came to getting Sadie's cooperation I might have more influence over her than Mum.

Mum wanted Sadie to drop her complaint against Mr Anderson and they were engaged in a tetchy to and fro about it. Mum said Mr Anderson clearly hadn't *deliberately* shared the confidential information with Sean. Sadie said he shouldn't have shared it with his wife either. Mum said that husbands and wives couldn't be expected not to talk to each other about their jobs. Sadie told her that was rubbish because lots of people with stressful jobs didn't have a husband or wife to offload on to and they seemed to manage.

Mr Jamieson told Sadie that he accepted there was a confidentiality issue to be looked at, but that her assault on Sean was a far more serious offence and one that he intended to address as a priority. And that he was going to suspend her.

As soon as he said that Sadie pushed back her chair and jumped from her seat, shouting that we were all in this together and that she was done listening to any of us.

'You're all pathetic!' she snapped. Then she told Mr Jamieson she was going to make an official complaint about the school to social services. 'And you're going to face disciplinary action for the way you run it,' she added angrily.

Mum and I nearly fell off our chairs. Even Mr Jamieson, who never usually gets ruffled, looked slightly taken aback.

'Sadie, that's enough!' Mum snapped, standing up along with her. It was the sternest I'd ever heard her when she was addressing my cousin.

'You're not my mum!' Sadie yelled. 'YOU can't tell me what to do!'

Mum just sighed. I have to say that she's always been good at ignoring any you're-not-my-mum missiles that get hurled at her when she's fostering.

'Sadie, everyone here is trying to help you. Please stop fighting us,' she persisted.

'You don't want to help me!' Sadie screamed. 'You just want to get rid of me!' And before anyone could stop her she was out through the door.

'Wait there. I'll see if I can get her back,' Mr Jamieson said, quickly following.

After he'd gone, Mum and I sat in shocked silence for a few moments. Mum had tears in her eyes.

'Oh, Mum.' I leaned across and put my arm around her.

After what seemed like forever, but was only about five minutes, Mr Jamieson finally came back. 'I'm afraid she's left the school,' he told us with a worried frown. 'She went out through the main gate. Hopefully she's on her way home.'

'I'd better go back and wait for her, then,' Mum said. 'I'll call social services to fill them in.' She met my gaze and gave me a little smile. 'Well, Poppy,' she said in a weak attempt at a joke, 'I guess this means the honeymoon period's over!'

Chapter Twenty-One

At home time all I knew was that I had to speak to Josh.

I texted him as I walked across the playground, but got no reply. Then I spotted him walking slowly out through the gates a short distance ahead of me, talking on his phone. As I caught up with him and waited for his conversation to end, I quickly picked up that he was speaking to Sean.

'How is he?' I asked after he'd finished the call.

'Nothing's broken, apparently. His mum's feeding him some soup and some painkillers the doctor prescribed and tucking him up in bed as we speak.'

'So he's OK?'

'Well, he's pretty upset about what happened. He says his mum and Leo are really angry with him for eavesdropping, never mind for blurting out *what* he overheard. Leo's got to go and see Mr Jamieson after school. How much further it goes will depend a bit on Sadie, I guess.' He paused. 'Leo's told Sean he has to keep away from Sadie in future – and he doesn't want him hanging out with her or *you* outside of school.'

I gulped. '*Me?*' I hadn't seen that one coming.

'Yeah ... Leo says you and Sadie are like sisters now and that Sean can't avoid her if he's still seeing you.'

'We are not like sisters!'

'Well, that's how Leo sees it, apparently. He knew the four of us were planning to go bowling together. That's never going to happen now, obviously.'

'Right ...' I felt stunned.

'You sound almost as disappointed as Sean,' Josh said in a teasing voice. He grinned. 'You do know that he fancies you, right?'

'Huh?' For a moment I wondered if I'd heard him correctly.

'You're on his Top Five Cutest Girls list.'

'Josh, don't be stupid!' I declared, scowling at him.

'I'm dead serious, Poppy! He asked me if I thought you'd go out with him.'

I just gaped at him. Mind you, I couldn't deny the flutter of excitement I felt as well.

'So would you?' Josh prompted me.

Would I? I really liked Sean, and I suppose I'd have to admit that I was enjoying his company more and more. But did I fancy him? Did I want to go out with him?

'That depends ...' I looked at Josh carefully, trying to work out what *he* thought about me dating his best friend. I was remembering what Anne-Marie had said about how you can't have a boyfriend *and* have a boy as your best friend because the two of them will get jealous of each other.

I didn't ask Josh what he thought about that because it was too embarrassing. But I did remind myself that no way was Anne-Marie always right about stuff like this.

Sadie wasn't back when I got home and Mum was starting to worry.

'Maybe we should go out and look for her,' she said.

'Where would we look, Mum? She could be anywhere. Just wait and she'll come back.'

Mum phoned Lenny, who said to give it a bit longer before we started worrying because Sadie had gone off on her own a lot of times before and so far she'd always returned the same day.

'I think I'll try her phone again,' Mum said after another half hour had gone by.

'I expect it's still switched off,' I warned her.

Mum tried it anyway and I was right.

I made her a cup of tea and got her to sit down. She refused the chocolate biscuits I put in front of her, which I knew meant she must be really nervous. When Mum's feeling upset she comfort eats like mad. It's only when she's truly scared about something that she can't eat anything. She can't sit still then either and she fidgets a lot like she was doing now.

'Mum, can I ask you something?' I said, thinking now was as good a time as any to bring this up.

'Of course.'

'What if you found out that you couldn't manage to look after both me and Sadie? Would you want me to go and live with Dad?' I hoped she wouldn't get upset with me for asking. I just needed to know the truth. Or rather, I needed to hear that if it ever came to a choice between Sadie and me, then she would choose me, no matter how many alternative homes I had available to me.

'What?' She was clearly taken aback by my question. 'Poppy, I can't imagine *why* you'd think you needed to ask that. I'd never want you to live full-time with your father instead of with me.'

'But what if me and Sadie don't *ever* get along? *She's* got nowhere else to go, has she? I have.'

'Poppy, you're my daughter! I would never take in another child if it meant that I couldn't keep you!'

'Not even Sadie?'

'Of course not even Sadie.'

'Oh.' I gave her a relieved smile. The way she said it left me in no doubt that she was speaking the truth.

But she clearly felt that she needed to say more. 'Poppy, you are my only child and my greatest gift and you must never forget that!' Then she added, 'But I see *all* the children we look after as gifts, no matter where they've come from or how long we get to keep them. You realise that, don't you?'

'Of course, Mum.' I understood what she was telling me. Yes, I was her only 'forever' child, which gave me the priority. But that didn't mean that all the children we fostered meant nothing to her.

Mum said solemnly, 'I see Sadie as a very special gift – and not one to be given up lightly.'

Not as lightly as you gave up Amy. The thought just popped into my head out of nowhere. *Stop it*, I told myself. *This isn't about Amy*. The Amy discussion can wait for another day.

'Maybe we *should* go out and look for Sadie,' I murmured. It was hard for me to view Sadie as a gift, but I realised even I was starting to worry a bit about where she had got to.

But it turned out we didn't have to look, because right at that moment our 'gift' came walking back in through the front door.

'I'm really tired and I'm going to lie down,' she said in a very quiet, very reasonable voice.

'Sadie, we need to talk about what happened at school today,' Mum said anxiously. 'Where did you go to? I was so worried!'

'I've just been walking around,' she said, avoiding eye contact with Mum. 'Listen, I've got a headache. We can talk later, right?' She went straight upstairs.

Mum still looked worried but she told me to take Sadie some paracetamol for her headache, while she phoned Lenny to let her know Sadie was back safely.

I walked into Sadie's room without bothering to knock and caught her texting. 'Who's that?' I asked.

'None of your business.' She quickly put down her phone where I couldn't see it. 'What's that?'

'Pills for your headache.'

'I don't need them.'

'I know. Cos you don't really have a headache, do you?' When she didn't say anything I added in as reasonable a voice as I could manage, 'I bet Sean has one hell of a headache. Why did you have to punch him, Sadie? He hadn't told a soul what he overheard about your dad.'

At least she had the decency to look a bit guilty. 'Yeah, well, I'm sorry, OK? I have this problem with my anger. That's one of the reasons I've been seeing Mrs Thomson … and I'm meant to count to ten and take deep breaths and stuff, but it's hard when people wind me up about my dad. I just see red.'

'Sean's not allowed to see either of us any more – you *or* me! Josh just told me.'

'Oops.'

OOPS? *Was that really all she could think of to say?*

'Sorry. Still … it'll just make your little romance all the more fun, won't it? You and Sean will just have to see each other in secret – like Romeo and Juliet.'

'Sadie, have you even *seen* that play? It's got the most tragic ending ever!'

'Has it? The only bit I know is where Juliet's on the balcony going "Romeo, Romeo, where the hell are you?"' She giggled.

What was wrong with her?

'Sadie, you are *so* annoying,' I burst out, losing my fight to stay calm. 'And what have you got against Sean? Even before you punched him, what you said to Anne-Marie about his dad was really horrible. It's like you think *you're* the only one who deserves sympathy!'

She had stopped giggling. 'I don't know what you're talking about.'

'You said it wasn't sad that his dad died!'

'I said it wasn't *that* sad! And it's not! I mean, at least his dad didn't *choose* to go off and leave him, did he?'

'Neither did yours!'

'No, but *she* did! She even wrote and said we should think of her as dead! But she wasn't dead! If she was, it wouldn't have been so bad!' Suddenly there were tears in her eyes.

'Sadie –' I hadn't realised until then which parent she'd been thinking about. 'Sadie ...' But I couldn't think of anything to say.

'Just go away and leave me alone!' she snapped. Her phone beeped as a text came through, and she promptly jumped up and shoved me out of her room.

I couldn't stop thinking about what Sadie had just said. It was true that if her mum had died then at least she'd have a story to tell that would earn her some sympathy. Instead she was too ashamed of what her mum had done to want to tell anyone about it. I understood now why she was so angry all the time. In fact, if I was her, then I'm pretty sure I'd be permanently angry too.

No wonder she felt abandoned all over again by her dad, and that she didn't really trust Mum yet, even though it sometimes seemed like she was trying to. And no wonder she was so short on sympathy for other people, especially people whose parents (or step-parents) clearly cared about them.

And I could totally see why she had befriended Alison – the one person who had been through something similar and really understood what she was going through.

I went to sleep that night thinking about what it must be like to actually *be* Sadie, and those were not happy thoughts at all.

Chapter Twenty-Two

The next two days of school passed in a bit of a haze while Sadie was suspended. Then came Thursday. It was Sadie's last day at home, and that afternoon Mum was bringing her in to a meeting with Mr Jamieson and Mrs Thomson. Her social worker was also going to be there. By that time Sadie had apologised to Sean and she had also dropped her complaint against Mr Anderson, thank goodness.

Anyway, straight after lunch we had English, and I thought I heard a few sniggers as I walked in. I looked sharply at Julia and Katy, who as usual were the ones laughing at me. Anne-Marie says they're just jealous because I'm friends with Josh, but I'm not so sure that's all it is. Though it's true Katy once asked me to ask Josh if he fancied her, and she hadn't been too chuffed when I'd had to report back that he didn't.

Mr Anderson was sitting at his desk reading a letter. As I walked past him I saw a pink envelope with hearts drawn on it lying open in front of him. I was curious, but I resisted the urge to try and get a closer look.

As I went to sit down, Evie Pennycook, who sits right at the front, asked, 'Who's your letter from, Mr Anderson?' which made a couple of the others start sniggering.

Our teacher ignored her as he folded the letter and replaced it in the envelope before putting it away and clapping his hands for silence. 'OK, let's get started, shall we?'

He had written some questions up on the whiteboard so I had no choice but to wear my glasses. I immediately felt self-conscious as I put them on. They really are very unflattering. I'd considered leaving them at home today, but the trouble is I can't really function at school without them. I couldn't wait for my new ones to be ready.

After I'd put them on I noticed Evie turning round to give me an amused look and I felt even more embarrassed. Were my glasses really that bad? In fact, I was a bit taken aback by the amount of amused glances that seemed to be aimed at me this afternoon. Eventually I took off my glasses and stuffed them into my schoolbag.

'What's question four?' I whispered to Anne-Marie.

She gave me a puzzled look as she whispered back, 'Why have you taken off your glasses?'

'Everyone's laughing at them.'

'I don't think it's your glasses they're laughing at. I think it's something to do with that letter.'

'Poppy ... Anne-Marie ... is there something you wish to share?' Mr Anderson said sternly.

At that comment, several more people started laughing.

'ENOUGH!' Mr Anderson sounded angrier than he usually does when our class gets disruptive, and we all quickly got back to work.

Later, as we were leaving the classroom, Mr Anderson asked me in a quiet voice to wait behind for a minute. For a crazy moment I thought he might be going to make some comment about my glasses too. But instead he waited until the room was empty before asking, 'Poppy, do you know anything about the letter that was on my desk this morning?'

'No,' I replied at once, shaking my head earnestly.

He nodded as he said, 'OK, then. It doesn't matter. You can go now.'

I left feeling puzzled. Why was he asking me and nobody else?

Out in the playground Katy and Julia came up to me, both of them sporting big fat grins. 'So, Poppy,' Julia began smugly. 'We didn't know you had such a mega-crush on Mr Anderson.'

'What?'

'Thing is,' Katy added, 'we've heard he goes for older women, not younger ones, so you probably haven't got much of a chance.' They both giggled like they thought they were the funniest double act on earth.

'Still, I'm sure he was flattered by your letter!'

'Yeah, Poppy ... what did you say in it exactly?'

They both started laughing hysterically again.

'Leave her alone!' It was Anne-Marie who rescued me – though I still hadn't worked out yet exactly what she was rescuing me *from*. 'Poppy, just ignore them. It's obvious you didn't write that letter.'

'What are you all talking about?' I asked as she pulled me away.

'I just spoke to Evie. She saw that letter Mr Anderson got just now. According to her, *you're* the one who wrote it.'

'*What?*'

'She couldn't read what it said but she saw your name at the bottom. Evie says it reeked of perfume.'

'I didn't write it!' I exclaimed in horror.

'I know that.' Anne-Marie frowned. 'You know, if Sadie was here I'd say it's just the sort of thing *she* would do and think was really funny.'

'Well, she isn't here.' I gritted my teeth. 'I bet it was Katy. Or Julia.' The two were out of earshot, halfway across the playground walking out of school together.

'I think it might have been both of them,' Anne-Marie said. 'They were both over at Mr Anderson's desk when I came into class. I was early and they were the only ones there.'

'I'm going to ask them!' I announced, hurrying to catch up with them before they disappeared through the main gate.

'Hey, Julia! Katy!' I called out sharply as I reached them just outside the school. 'I want to talk to you!'

As they stopped walking and turned to face me, I said breathlessly, 'I know you wrote that letter to Mr Anderson!'

'A *love* letter, to be exact,' Julia said, smirking. 'I'm sure you'd blush if you read it – seeing as how you blush so easily.'

'Yeah,' Katy added. 'You know you can get this green make-up to put on your face to help with that. My big sister tried it. It's supposed to counteract the pinkness or something.'

'I'm going to tell Mr Anderson it was you,' I said, making to go back into school. Just talking about blushing is enough to make me start these days and I wanted to get away before it happened.

'Hey, it's very rude to turn your back on a person when they're talking to you,' Katy called out, giving my hair a sharp tug from behind.

'OUCH!'

Julia was grinning. 'You want to watch it or you might find your hair getting accidently chopped off.'

'Yeah,' said Katy. 'All it takes is for someone to bring a pair of scissors into school!'

I glared at them, feeling my adrenalin level rise even though I was fairly sure they were bluffing.

Suddenly I heard a familiar voice behind me. 'Did you just threaten my cousin?'

It was Sadie. I hadn't expected her to still be here after her meeting. I couldn't see Mum, but I guessed she must be somewhere nearby too.

Maybe because of the grim tone of voice Sadie used, or maybe just because of the reputation she had, Julia and Katy immediately stopped grinning.

'So what's going on, Poppy?' Sadie asked me without taking her eyes off either of them.

I quickly told her about the letter.

Sadie glared at the other two. 'Nobody makes fun of *my* family.'

'Sadie, it's OK,' I said, trying to calm her down.

'No, it's not. What was in that letter, Julia?'

'It was just a joke,' Julia started to say, but Katy quickly put her hand in her pocket and pulled out a sheet of paper. 'Here. This is the first draft. Read it yourself.'

Sadie read it first, then passed it to me.

Dear Mr Anderson (or can I call you Leo?),

I am writing to let you know that I didn't mean what I said before about your bum being big. I think you have a lovely bum. You are definitely the cutest teacher in our school and you have a totally sexy voice that makes me go all tingly up my spine.

LOVE AND KISSES,

Your biggest admirer,

Poppy

'Urgh!' I exclaimed, sure that my face must have turned beetroot red.

Sadie looked serious. 'OK, tonight the two of you can write another letter telling Mr Anderson that one was from you.'

'And what if we don't?' Julia snapped.

Sadie took just one step towards her. 'Julia, you do know *why* I got suspended, don't you?'

'If you punch *us*, you'll get expelled,' Katy said coldly.

Sadie just shrugged. 'I honestly don't care! I didn't even want to come to this school in the first place!'

We watched the two exchange uncertain glances before turning away and leaving us together.

'Those two had better not mess with either of us from now on,' Sadie said fiercely. 'Come on. Your mum's waiting for us in the car. She couldn't find a big enough parking space near the school so she ended up driving miles up the road. She told me to come and fetch you.'

As we set off along the road together I asked doubtfully, 'Do you *really* think they'll tell Mr Anderson that letter was from them?'

Sadie shrugged. 'If they don't it'll just give me a good excuse to whack them both.'

'Sadie, you can't just go around hitting people whenever they make you angry.'

'Why not? They were threatening *you*! Or don't you mind getting your hair cut off?'

'They wouldn't really have done that.'

'Fine. So in that case I wouldn't really have punched them.' She paused. 'Anyway, don't mention it.'

'Mention what?'

'I mean, you're very welcome, Poppy.'

We heard a horn tooting and looked over to see Mum double parked on the other side of the road. Obviously she'd got fed up waiting for us.

'Thank you, Sadie,' I finally said as we crossed the road together. 'Thank you for standing up for me just now. I really do appreciate it. And thank you for saying I'm your family.'

She nodded curtly. 'No problem. And anyway ... you *are*.'

Chapter Twenty-Three

The next day brought both good news and bad.

The good news was that Julia and Katy confessed to their letter-writing prank and were instructed to write *me* a letter of apology.

The bad news was that when I got home from school Mum told me that tomorrow's visit to Amy had been postponed for yet *another* week because now Amy's new sister had just come down with chickenpox.

So on Saturday morning Sadie and I stayed at home helping Mum in the house and doing our homework. When Mum went upstairs just after lunch to make a couple of phone calls, Sadie said she would load the dishwasher if I wanted to go and get on with the English essay I'd been struggling with all morning. (Sadie had already done hers while she was suspended.)

About twenty minutes later as I finally finished my

homework I thought I heard the front door close. Mum was still on the phone in the bedroom so I went downstairs calling out Sadie's name. In the kitchen the lunch things had been cleared and there was a note on the table which said, *Back later. Sadie.*

I ran to the front door, flung it open and spotted Sadie hurrying away down our street. Where was she sneaking off to without telling anyone?

I frowned. Today was the day Alison had mentioned in her text. *Be careful,* she had said.

I don't know what possessed me to follow her without even taking my phone with me or leaving another note for Mum. I think I had some idea I would catch up with her and talk her into coming back before Mum even got off the phone. Anyway I wasn't thinking straight as I grabbed my jacket from the banister and raced off down our road after her. I decided not to let her know I was following until I found out where she was going.

She headed straight past the park and along the road towards the little row of shops where the second-hand bookshop is.

I kept watch from a safe distance as she disappeared inside the cafe. Was she meeting someone there or what?

I knew I couldn't wait outside forever because Mum would be worried when she discovered we were missing. I either needed to return home or borrow a phone to give her a call.

Just as I was debating what to do a familiar voice called out my name and I turned to see Sean coming out of the estate agent's where his mum works. I couldn't help remembering what Josh had said about him fancying me and I felt myself flushing and feeling horribly awkward. Out of school uniform he looked a bit older and a lot cooler, despite the bruise on his face. His boyish grin was just the same.

'I brought Mum her keys that she left at home *again* and now she wants me to fetch her a coffee from the cafe,' he said, talking rapidly as if he was a bit nervous too. 'So what are you doing here? Looking for a really weird birthday gift again?'

'No,' I answered. 'Sean, are you going into the cafe right now?'

'Yeah. Why? Want to come with me and get a Coke or something?' Forbidden or not, he didn't seem at all bothered about hanging out with me.

'Oh … no …' I lowered my voice as I continued, 'Sadie's in there. I'm sure she's planning to do something dodgy and I'm trying to follow her without her seeing me.' I quickly reminded him about the text we'd been discussing just before she'd punched him.

Sean looked amused. 'And here's me thinking I was going to have a dead boring Saturday. Listen, I'll go and get that takeout coffee for my mum, and while I'm in there I'll see what I can find out, shall I?'

'OK, but be careful what you say this time.' The last thing I wanted was for him to get punched on the nose again.

By the time Sean came out of the cafe – with Sadie – I had gone to hide inside the bookshop. The bookshop owner was giving me sharp looks as I hovered by the window pretending to read a musty old book I'd picked up, which I suddenly saw was all about fly-fishing.

Sean was carrying a takeaway coffee and Sadie had a can of Coke and they chatted for a minute before Sadie walked off.

I quickly put back the book and went outside to meet Sean.

'She actually told me again she was sorry for punching me,' he said. 'And you know what – I'm starting to believe her! She was in there just now asking how to get to Percy

Street. Apparently she went there straight from school before, and she doesn't know the way from this direction. Says she's going to see a friend.'

'Anne-Marie lives in Percy Street,' I said at once.

'So maybe Anne-Marie asked her round?'

'This is the day she told us Anne-Marie and her family were going to visit her aunt – remember?' I was getting a bad feeling now – a very bad feeling … 'Come on. Let's follow her.' Then I felt myself blushing as I realised the assumption I'd made. 'Oh … sorry … of course, you don't have to come with me.'

'No, it's OK. I'll come after I've delivered Mum's coffee. You go after her and I'll catch you up. But Poppy, what is it you think she's about to *do*, exactly?'

When I told him I thought she might be going to let out all of Anne-Marie's animals from their cages, he just gaped at me in disbelief. 'We're talking about Sadie, right? Animal-loving Sadie who wants to ban all non-living fur and feathers from the school premises?'

I nodded.

'And you really think she's going to do *that*? You don't think she's just going to padlock herself to the rabbit hutch or something!'

I knew he was trying to cheer me up but I couldn't

seem to even squeeze out a smile. 'No. That's why I have to catch her in the act and talk her out of it.'

'Well, you go ahead. I'll see you in a minute!'

I walked on, keeping a good distance between us. If she spotted me I was afraid she would just deny everything and postpone the whole thing to a time when she knew I wasn't around.

Sean caught up with me on the other side of the railway bridge. Sadie had just turned the corner into Anne-Marie's street. While we were relatively safe from being spotted I asked Sean if I could borrow his phone to text Mum, but in the end I couldn't think what to say so I just handed it back to him to switch off.

'Now I'm breaking another one of Leo's rules,' he told me. *'Always have your phone switched on when you're out and about.'* He grinned. 'You know he worries far more than Mum about that kind of thing. We had much more freedom when it was just her.'

At his mention of Leo I remembered there was something I badly wanted to ask him. 'Sean, is it true what Josh said ... that you're not supposed to hang out with *me* outside school any more, just because I'm Sadie's cousin?'

Sean pulled a face. 'Yeah ... Leo says Sadie's a

troublemaker and even though he knows you're not, he doesn't want *me* getting drawn into whatever trouble Sadie draws *you* into.'

'*What* trouble?' I said dismissively.

He laughed as he replied, 'Well, I guess the sort that's happening right now!'

Chapter Twenty-Four

We watched from across the road as Sadie walked up to the front door of Anne-Marie's house and stood there ringing the bell as if she was calling in for her. After a moment or two she walked confidently round to the side gate.

'Come on,' I said to Sean. 'Time we joined her. We'll just act all normal, like we're calling in for Anne-Marie too.'

'Josh always said you weren't as timid as you seemed,' Sean said, grinning. 'You're actually pretty feisty, aren't you?'

I rolled my eyes at that.

As we stood in front of Anne-Marie's house there was no sign of anyone being at home and I quickly tugged Sean towards the side entrance.

We entered the back garden and straight away I saw

Sadie letting out the guinea pigs.

'Sadie!' I hissed, and she turned round, looking startled.

'What are *you* doing here?' she snapped.

'Sadie, you can't do this!'

'*You* followed me from the cafe, didn't you?' Sadie was glaring at Sean. 'You'd better leave now if you don't want another punch on the nose. *Both* of you!'

I stepped forward, struggling to keep calm. I knew I had to if I wanted to get her to listen. 'Sadie, what are you trying to do exactly?'

'What does it look like?' she retorted. 'I'm freeing these poor animals.'

'Sadie, listen!' I said. 'This isn't the same as what you did at Linda's. These aren't fur coats! They're live animals!'

Sadie snorted. 'Thanks, Poppy, but I *can* actually tell the difference.'

'Sadie, these are just pets! They don't even know *how* to live in the wild,' I tried again.

'Yeah,' Sean joined in. 'All you're doing is killing off a bunch of innocent little furries!'

'I'm not *killing* them – I'm giving them a chance to have a proper life!' Sadie snapped.

'A very *short* proper life!' Sean argued. 'I'd say most of

them will be dead by tonight. They'll either end up as roadkill or the foxes'll get them. And that's if they don't get squashed by a train first.' As if on cue a train rattled by along the tracks that ran behind the back garden fence, sounding alarmingly close.

'Better to have one day of freedom than a lifetime trapped in a cage,' Sadie shouted above the noise.

'But these are *pet* rabbits!' Sean protested once the train had passed. 'They've *always* lived in a cage. They probably like it!'

'Oh, so you can talk to the animals now, can you, Doctor Doolittle?' Sadie said.

'Don't be daft –'

'Well, how do *you* know what they like?'

'Sadie, the rabbits have got babies!' I reminded her as she took a determined step towards one of the big wooden hutches.

'I know. How would *you* like to be born in a cage and spend your whole life there?'

'But Sadie, *these* baby rabbits won't get any life at all if you let them out. It's not like they've even got a burrow to protect them. The mothers will probably get scared and run off and the babies will be terrified.'

'Yes,' said Sean. 'First they're going to be petrified and

then they're going to have really disgusting deaths being ripped apart by some fox.'

Sadie looked uncertain – and a bit like she might be going to throw up – and I made sure I took advantage of the moment. 'Sadie, if you leave now I promise I'll set up that zoo debate for you,' I offered. 'I'm chairing it, remember. Just before it starts I'll announce that we're doing the zoo one instead of school uniforms. You'll be able to get your point across to the whole assembly hall and change loads of people's minds about zoos – and you won't be hurting any real animals.'

It was a good argument and I had definitely got Sadie's attention. Suddenly Sean said, 'Hey! The man next door is looking out of his upstairs window. I think he's seen us.'

Sadie ignored him, still looking at me fiercely. 'You'll really fix that debate?'

I nodded. 'Absolutely. You can argue against zoos all you like.'

'You promise?'

'Promise.'

'OK.' Just for a second I thought she looked relieved as she cast a last glance over the rabbit hutches, where two of the babies were playing together in the straw. She turned to go, calling back to Sean and me as she reached the gate, 'Come on, then!'

'In a minute,' I called back. 'I want to catch the guinea pigs first.'

'Well, it's your funeral.' And she disappeared from view.

'Sean, did you really see the neighbour?' I asked him the second she'd gone.

'No. I keep expecting to though. Come on. Let's find those guinea pigs and get out of here.'

'Their names are Elizabeth and Mr Darcy. They get to run around in the garden quite a bit so they're used to it. They like eating dandelion leaves. Look. There's Mr Darcy.' I went over to him slowly, making friendly noises before I managed to scoop him up and put him back in his enclosure.

Sean was looking around for the second guinea pig but not having much luck. 'We'd better go, Poppy. I know I made it up about that neighbour seeing us, but I really don't want to get caught here.'

'We can't just leave Elizabeth. Anything could happen to her.'

'Listen, I don't know about Elizabeth, but I know what's going to happen to *me* if I'm picked up for trespassing!'

'You can leave if you want,' I said as I stubbornly went to check under another bush.

'I'm not even meant to be hanging out with you,' Sean continued as he came over to help me. 'You do realise this is just proving Leo right about you being a really bad influence?'

'I just said you could go, didn't I?'

But he didn't go, and we searched together for another half an hour before Sean suddenly spotted the missing guinea pig in a patch of long grass in the neighbour's garden. All I had to do was climb over the (thankfully low) fence to fetch her.

'All present and accounted for now, right?' Sean said after we'd returned Elizabeth to Mr Darcy and checked that their enclosure was escape proof.

'Yes, thank goodness.'

'Good. So let's go!'

We sneaked out through the side gate and started walking back together along the road.

'I wonder where Sadie went,' I said.

'Don't worry about *her*,' Sean grunted. 'If you want to worry about someone, worry about *me*.' He had switched on his phone and he showed me the missed calls from his mother and also from Mr Anderson. There were several texts, including one from his sister that said, *THEY KNOW U R AWOL!*

'Sorry,' I said guiltily. 'This is all my fault.'

'No, it's not. I didn't *have* to come with you.'

'So ... why did you?' I couldn't help asking. 'I guess you must really like animals, right?'

He gave me a cheeky grin. 'Animals are OK – but I really like you!'

'Oh.' I felt myself flushing bright red and I couldn't look at him. 'Listen, I didn't mean to get you in trouble,' I mumbled.

'Hey, it's OK. I'm always in trouble of some kind or another. Mum calls me the trouble magnet.'

'Does she?' I paused, sneaking a look at his face again. 'You know, you don't talk about your mum as much as you talk about Leo.'

He shrugged. 'Oh, well ... I take her more for granted, I guess. She's the one who's always been around. I never have bothered much about what she thinks of me. Whereas with Leo ... well, I guess I worry more about ... well ... about ...'

'About not disappointing him?' I suggested. At that moment I felt as if we were perfectly in tune with each other – like we were on exactly the same wavelength.

'Because that's how it is for me too,' I continued. 'Dad's the one I'm always trying to make proud of me. I don't live with him and I wish I could see him a bit more than I do. Mum's the one I take for granted. At least –' I broke off abruptly as I realised something.

I used to take her for granted. Before Sadie came to live with us.

Sean's large dark-brown eyes were full of sympathy. He also had really gorgeous thick dark eyelashes, I realised. 'So do you think you might want to come bowling with me sometime, or to the cinema or something?' he asked in an ever-so-casual tone.

'Sure,' I croaked, cursing my voice for not doing what I wanted it to. 'But aren't you banned from seeing me ever again?'

'Not *ever again* – just until Leo calms down. Don't worry. He always does. He's just mad because this whole thing with Sadie made him look stupid at work.' He frowned. 'I do feel bad about that. I can be so dumb sometimes.'

'I don't think you're dumb,' I blurted out. 'And I think it's really sweet the way you care about him so much.'

Uh-oh. Why did I go and say that? Now his ears are going red.

'You know what?' he retaliated with a bit of a grin. '*I* think it's sweet the way you just blurt out really uncool stuff that nobody else would ever say. It makes you ... well ... different from just about any other girl I know!'

We chatted about all kinds of stuff the rest of the way back.

'So what are you going to tell your mum about where you were?' I asked as we arrived outside the estate agent's.

'I'll just say I met you and decided to hang out with you for a bit. I won't mention Sadie!'

'But you're not meant to be seeing me outside of school. Aren't you going to get in a lot of trouble?'

'It's OK. Mum'll probably leave it to Leo, and Leo will just be all stern and launch into his "you're pushing the boundaries again, kiddo" speech. Apparently that's what you do when you're testing out a new stepdad. Leo's been reading loads of parenting books since he married Mum and he's got quite into the whole psychology thing ...'

I giggled. Actually what he'd said sounded quite similar to the kind of stuff Mum and Lenny are always talking about.

'Well, thanks for coming with me,' I said. 'And for

staying to help me catch Elizabeth. I might still be there looking if you hadn't spotted her.'

He grinned. 'Next time remember to bring your glasses.'

'Oh, did I tell you I'm getting new ones?'

'Cool.'

'With oval frames.'

'Right.'

I suddenly wondered if he'd noticed I have a square face.

Chapter Twenty-five

To my surprise, Sadie was waiting for me at the corner of our street. She was on her own.

'I sent you a text to see where you were and Aunt Kathy called me back,' she said. 'Boy, is she mad! What an idiot, leaving your phone behind!'

Ignoring that, I said, 'Listen, she's going to want to know where we've been. Sean's promised not to tell and neither will I, but we have to make sure our stories match up.'

Sadie looked incredulous. 'You're actually going to cover for me? Are you sure? You'd probably get in a lot less trouble if you told your mum the truth.' Her phone beeped and she looked down at it quickly. 'Alison again. Hang on a minute.'

I waited while she texted back. 'Alison knew what you were doing today, didn't she?' I murmured.

'Yeah. She thought it was a bit daft, to be fair ... I told her about your offer to change the debate and she thinks it's a really good idea. But she says she can't change her coach tickets so she needs to leave tomorrow night. Did I tell you she and Joe are leaving town? He's just got himself a job in the Midlands and –'

'I already saw that message she sent telling *you* to meet her at the bus station,' I said. 'Tell me the truth, Sadie. Are you going with them?'

Sadie sighed. 'I'm thinking about it. Look, you can't tell anyone, OK? She only asked me last week. She's almost eighteen now, and Joe's a year older, so she says they'll be able to look after me and we can tell everybody I'm her sister.'

'But that's stupid!' I protested. 'Social services will look for you and you'll all get into loads of trouble.'

'Alison says they won't find us. She says only Joe's brother knows where they're going and he won't tell anyone.' She paused. 'And it's not like anyone's going to bust a gut searching for me, is it? Not with Dad in prison.'

'What are you talking about? *Mum* will bust a gut!'

'Will she? She'll probably think I'm behaving exactly like my mother. And she didn't go after *her*, did she?'

'That wasn't the same! Your mum was an adult when she ran off … Oh, and by the way, I know Mum didn't steal you when you were little. She wanted to have you live with us but your dad wouldn't let her. I don't know what your dad told you, but mine says that your dad got scared because he thought Mum was trying to take you away from him. That's why he stopped us seeing you.'

'You *told* your dad what I said?'

'You never said not to. You just said I couldn't tell Mum!' I paused. 'You made that kidnapping story up, didn't you? Your dad didn't tell you that at all!'

She swallowed, looking a bit guilty. 'So does Aunt Kathy know?'

'What you said about her? Shouldn't think so, since Dad and her never speak to each other. But Sadie, you're wrong about Mum not looking for you if you ran away! Mum thinks you belong with *us* now. She thinks she's been given this amazing second chance to look after you. She told me she sees you as a gift.'

'A *gift*?' Sadie gave a dry little laugh. 'Well, that makes a change from feeling like some piece of old junk that nobody wants.' She was speaking in a jokey voice as if she didn't care, but she didn't fool me. I felt like she was showing me her true feelings without even realising it.

I wanted to quash those feelings with all my might, but the trouble was, I couldn't think of a single appropriate thing to say. So I made do with something that sounded utterly daft even as it came out of my mouth. 'You know, you're a bit like something in a charity shop. One person throws you out because they don't want you any more, but another person comes along and buys you and thinks you're absolutely brilliant!'

Sadie snorted. 'Thanks for that example, Poppy. I feel so much better!'

'I know that probably didn't come out right, but I just meant –'

'You meant I'm like that awful loo roll cover your mum thinks is so wonderful, right?'

'NO! Well, only in the sense that –'

'Poppy, just shut up, OK?'

'OK.' But I think maybe it did help a tiny bit because she seemed pretty relaxed as we walked the rest of the way home.

Mum opened the front door before we'd even reached it.

'Mum, I'm sorry,' I blurted out as she hugged me tightly.

She quickly pulled back and held me at arm's length. 'Poppy, I've been so worried.'

I vaguely registered the fact that she wasn't even trying to hug Sadie as I continued, 'I know I shouldn't have gone off like that but it's not like we weren't planning to come back. Sadie left you that note. I should have left you one too. I'm sorry.'

'I just assumed the note was from both of you,' Mum said. 'I thought Sadie must have persuaded you to go with her.'

Something about the way she said it made me turn to look at Sadie, who glanced at me as if to say, 'Told you so. *You're* the one she cares about.'

'Sadie didn't know I was following her,' I said. 'I wanted to see where she was going. Then I … I … I guess I lost track of the time.' That bit sounded false even to me.

Mum suddenly turned to Sadie. 'I found your rucksack under the bed,' she said coolly.

Sadie looked uncomfortable. 'I wasn't … I mean, I'm not … It was more of a just-in-case thing … not a definite plan.'

'Really?' Mum was giving her a long, hard stare. Then she snapped, 'Go up to your rooms now, both of you.'

As soon as we got upstairs I followed Sadie into her bedroom and shut the door behind me. I had to talk to

219

her. 'I thought you said you hadn't decided yet whether or not to go with Alison?'

Sadie let out a sigh. 'I haven't. I only packed my rucksack last night because I was feeling so angry. It's not completely packed. My toothbrush is still in the bathroom and I haven't even packed Bugsy.'

'Bugsy?'

She felt under her pillow and pulled out a small scruffy toy rabbit I hadn't seen before. 'Dad gave him to me when I was little.'

'You know if you go with Alison your dad's going to be really upset,' I said on an impulse, watching how she absent-mindedly cuddled the grubby toy against her chest.

I didn't expect the reaction I got.

'Good! He should be upset! How could he be so stupid?' she exploded, letting the toy rabbit drop out of her hand on to the bed. Then she just sat down, as if all the energy had gone out of her. 'He isn't even DANGEROUS! The lawyer said he wouldn't go to prison. They've got no RIGHT to shut him up inside some horrid little prison cell, treating him like he's some ... some ...'

'*Animal?*' I ventured softly.

She looked at me and I saw tears come to her eyes.

We sat in silence for quite a long time after that. I understood then how mixed up her feelings were about her dad and how she felt both angry with him and sorry for him at the same time. And I saw that even though he'd let her down in a really big way she still loved him. Finally she said, 'You know, in his last letter he said he was hoping to get moved to an open prison soon ... what do you think *they're* like?'

I shrugged. 'I don't know, but it sounds better. More like a safari park than a zoo, maybe?' It was a bit of a risky joke but to my relief she smiled.

Then I had an idea. 'I know. Let's go online and find out.'

So that afternoon while Mum stayed downstairs, too angry to speak to either of us, Sadie and I stayed in her room with our eyes glued to our phones as we researched all we could about open prisons. And I have to say Sadie looked much happier when we were done.

Intermittently throughout the afternoon Sadie got texts from Alison, and gradually she told me a bit more about her. She said that in the past she had always looked up to her – idolised her even – but that their relationship was changing. More recently she had started to question her a lot more, and it sounded like Alison had been finding that difficult to cope with. 'She keeps telling me I'm getting way too cocky and she's started smacking me if I contradict her in front of the others. It's like she's trying to be my mum, sorting me out with a clip round the ear. Joe thinks it's comical – calls it Alison "going all maternal" on me.'

'That's not maternal!' I protested. 'Mum would *never* hit you!'

'You sure about that? Cos just now she looked fit to flatten both of us,' Sadie pointed out with a grin. 'In fact, maybe you'd better go to your own room before she catches you in here and thinks I've led you astray again.'

'Hitting you isn't right, Sadie.'

Just as I said that we heard Mum out on the landing. I jumped up off the bed but it was too late to escape.

As Mum opened the door I was about to speak, but Sadie beat me to it. 'Aunt Kathy, I really am sorry for going off like that. I used to do it all the time when I lived with Dad. I know I shouldn't do it here though.'

'And the rucksack?' Mum asked sharply.

'It's like I said – I only packed that last night cos I was angry. I really don't want to leave.'

'Yes, Mum, remember how Amy used to pack that little rucksack and threaten to run away every time she got unhappy?' I said.

'It's hardly the same thing, Poppy!'

'*Why* isn't it? You always said Amy wasn't really planning to leave. You said she didn't have anywhere else to go. You said she just needed to know that *we* wouldn't let her go.'

Mum sighed. 'I'm sure Sadie must have worked out by now that I don't want her to run away.'

'I don't want her to either,' I added swiftly.

That surprised Mum, I could tell. 'Well, that's good to hear, Poppy, but the trouble is, it might not matter what *we* want any more.'

'How come?'

'Social services have to decide what to do after I tell them what happened today. And yes, I *do* have to tell them! You simply can't wander off whenever you feel like it without telling me where you're going. Now go back to your own room, Poppy. Tomorrow you're both grounded.' She gave us a stern glare as she left us.

But I still didn't go back to my room.

As another text came in on Sadie's phone I said, 'You *have* to tell Alison you're not going with her.'

'I can't. Not yet. I know how badly she wants me to go, and, well … she's been like family to me for such a long time …'

'But she *hits* you and … and …'

'It doesn't matter,' she said firmly. 'I know if I'm ever in real trouble, I can call her and she'll come straight away.'

'But Mum will do that too if you give her a chance!'

She sighed. 'But what if social services don't let me stay here? You heard what your mum said.'

'They *will* let you if you quit running off the whole time!'

'I don't know … it's true I don't need Alison as much any more, but I've never thought before about how she might still need *me* …'

'Why don't you just tell Mum all this?' I suggested. 'She might be able to help Alison too.'

But Sadie shook her head. 'Alison will be eighteen in a few months. She wants a fresh start without any adults interfering. We can't tell your mum anything, Poppy!'

Chapter Twenty-Six

Sunday was a weird day, and Sadie and I stayed in our rooms for the first half of it. I knew Sadie was still trying to decide what to do about Alison.

In the afternoon Mum started sorting out some photos of Amy to put in an album and she asked if I wanted to come downstairs and help. All being well, Mum and I were due to visit Amy in her new home next weekend.

'Mum, do *you* think Amy's parents are going to let us keep seeing her?' I couldn't stop myself asking for the zillionth time. We still hadn't received an answer and Lenny had recently reported back to us that they were still undecided.

Mum sighed. 'I honestly don't know what to think, Poppy. And before you ask, I don't know why they're taking so long to decide either. Perhaps they're waiting to see how our visit goes first.'

'I can't bear the thought of never seeing her again, Mum.'

She sighed again. 'I know, darling.'

As I picked up a photo of Amy and me in the park (taken only a few weeks ago) I asked, 'Is it really bad of me to wish that the Wilsons *hadn't* come along when they did?'

Mum didn't say anything straight away. Then she said softly, 'Of course not. It's important to be honest about how you feel.' She stopped at that, which surprised me a bit. I knew I was being selfish to wish away Amy's perfect new family, and I'd expected Mum to tell me so. Even if it was in her softly-softly, round-the-houses sort of way.

So I felt encouraged to continue as tears sprang to my eyes. 'Mum, I don't want you to get mad if I ask you this but ... I've been wondering ... How come you care so much about Sadie when you've only known her – this time round, I mean – for a couple of *weeks* ... and yet Amy was here for almost a whole *year* and you just ... well ... *let her go?*'

Mum gazed at me. '*Let her go?*'

'You could have tried to adopt her.'

'Poppy, you always knew we weren't going to be her forever family.'

'Yes, but we *could* have been. You even said "we'll see" that time when I asked you about adopting her!'

'Oh, Poppy ...' I had her full attention now. 'Yes, she was the first child ... first *foster-child*,' she corrected herself quickly, 'that I've even *considered* adopting. But then the Wilsons came along and I immediately knew it would be better for Amy to go to them. It just felt ... well ... *right*.'

'Cos they're black and we're not, I suppose!' I snapped before I could stop myself.

Mum frowned. 'Come on, Poppy. It's not just because they *look* like they could be her birth family! They have much more to offer her than we do in every respect.'

'Well, if they're so perfect, why can't they see how important it is for us to keep in touch with her?' I demanded.

'Poppy, whatever they decide it will be because they think it's the best thing for *Amy*.'

'Letting us keep in touch *is* the best thing for Amy! How can anyone not see that?'

Mum sounded tired as she continued, 'It's been a more difficult loss for you this time, Poppy ... I'm sorry about that ... That's one of the reasons I think it might work well if Sadie lived with us ...'

'We'd have to stop our other fostering, you mean?'

'Yes. Actually I think I'm going to take a break from it for a while, irrespective of what social services decide about Sadie.'

'But you do still really *want* Sadie to live with us, don't you?'

'I'd like to offer her a home until her father gets out of prison, yes,' Mum said. 'If we can manage her behaviour, I mean.' She paused. 'But I don't want our house turned into a battleground. It all depends on whether you two girls are willing to give each other a chance.'

After that I thought really hard about everything: about Amy and me; about Sadie and me; about Sadie and Alison.

Finally I went upstairs to speak to Sadie.

I found her on her bed texting away as usual. 'Alison?'

She nodded and carried on texting.

'You know what I've been thinking?' I said. 'I'm thinking that if you really want her to have a fresh start, then you *can't* go with her. Because how is she going to support you as well as herself? You're going to be a huge burden even if she can't see that yet. The only way she can have a fresh start without feeling like she's abandoned you is for you to tell her you don't *want* to go.'

When I'd finished I was a bit taken aback that Sadie had clearly been listening. In fact, she was even nodding.

'I need to think about it some more,' she murmured. 'About what's best for her as well as for me. But whatever I decide, I have to go to the bus station tonight and tell her to her face.'

'If you're going there to say goodbye, Mum might take you,' I said. 'If you explain everything to her.'

'No need. I'll just slip out. It's easier that way.'

'But when she finds out you're gone she's going to be really mad. And if social services find out …'

'I'll be careful. I've snuck out loads of times at home without getting caught.'

I pulled a face. 'Well, good luck with that.' Because I knew for a fact that Mum was going to be watching us like a hawk for the rest of the day.

As I sat on the sofa with Mum later that evening I kept sneaking looks at my watch, wondering if Sadie was really going to try and slip out to the bus station.

She had already sent Alison a text telling her she wasn't going to be coming with her but that she would come to say goodbye. Alison had texted back telling her to bring her stuff with her just in case she changed her mind at the last moment.

'But you're not going to, are you?' I'd asked in alarm.

'Change my mind? Of course not.'

'Or take your stuff?'

'Or take my stuff,' she said firmly.

'Not even that toy rabbit?'

She was looking at me like I was potty. 'I just told you *no*, didn't I?'

I nodded, but it didn't change the fact that I was still scared about the hold Alison seemed to have on her.

Mum and I were watching the last part of a detective thriller on TV, and as far as I knew Sadie was chilling out in her bedroom. At nine o'clock the ads came on and Mum went through to the kitchen to make a cup of tea.

'HEY!' I heard Mum exclaim.

I jumped up and found her glaring at Sadie, whom she had caught trying to leave our house by the back door.

'Where do you think *you're* going?' Mum asked in a deceptively quiet voice.

Sadie seemed frozen to the spot. 'I was just going out for a little while,' she muttered. I have to say she had never sounded more pathetic.

'Right, that's it!' Mum pushed past her, slammed the back door shut and locked it. 'If you want to go then you can! But you can leave by the front door! I'm phoning your social worker right now and she can sort this out! I can't be responsible for you any more!'

'But Mum, she only wants to say goodbye to her friend who's leaving on the coach tonight!' I blurted out.

Mum turned on me. 'You *knew* about this?'

'Well, yes … just that she wanted to say goodbye and … and this friend is really important to her, Mum.'

Mum looked at me angrily. 'And that makes it OK for both of you to treat me like I'm *not* important, I suppose!'

'No, Mum –'

She cut me off, turning to glare some more at Sadie. 'OK, miss, let's deal with *you* first. Right now I don't *care* about your reasons for sneaking out of this house yet again. All that matters to me is this – if you want to live in this house with me as your guardian then I need to know where you are at all times. *No exceptions.* And if you can't agree to that then you can't live here.' She paused to catch her breath. 'So *you* choose, Sadie. Because if you walk out on us to go and see your friend then I will phone social services and tell them to meet you at the bus station. And I'll pack your stuff and tell your social worker to come and collect it because you won't be coming back here again!'

There was an awful silence. Then Sadie said hoarsely, 'You don't want me –'

'No, I *do* want you!' Mum interrupted her angrily. 'So don't use *that* as an excuse. I want you to stay with us and so does Poppy. If you leave then it's because *you* want to. It's you who'll be making that choice.'

Sadie suddenly looked shivery. 'And if I don't go? If I just … go back upstairs?'

'Then you can go straight to bed and I'll be grounding you for the entire week!' Mum snapped.

'But –'

'It's your choice, Sadie,' Mum repeated. 'I can't let you stay here if I can't keep you safe and I can't keep you safe if I don't have any control over you.'

Sadie opened her mouth to speak, then closed it again. She started to cry silently. Mum didn't go to comfort her but just stood looking at her expectantly.

Finally Sadie walked out of the kitchen into the hall, paused for a split second by the front door, then started to climb the stairs.

Mum looked relieved, but her tone of voice was still firm as she called after her, 'You can call your friend to say goodbye if you want. After that I'm confiscating your phone until I feel I can trust you again.'

'Mum –' I whispered, at which point my mother turned her furious gaze on me and pointed silently in the direction of the stairs.

'Bed, Poppy. NOW!'

I gulped. She was mad all right.

Chapter Twenty-Seven

I didn't see Sean until lunchtime on Monday when he was standing in the canteen queue with Josh. I was pretty flattered when he spotted me and left the queue to come and say hello.

'So … how's everything?' I asked him, noting that his face didn't look nearly as bad now.

He reached up and touched his nose self-consciously. 'Oh … you know. Still in one piece.'

I gave him a small awkward smile, glad that the bruising was almost gone. 'So were they mad at you on Saturday?'

'Fairly! I'm grounded for the next week, but there's good news too! Mum thinks that if they forbid me doing *everything* then this is just the start of me sneaking around behind their backs all the time like *she* did as a teenager. Anyway they argued a bit but Mum eventually got Leo

234

to see things her way. So now they're saying that since you're "such a nice girl", and you can't help who your cousin is, I'm allowed to see you outside school after all!'

I felt my cheeks going a bit pink with pleasure. 'That's brilliant!'

'I knew he'd come round. I mean, he knows *you're* not a troublemaker. I just never expected Mum to get involved.' He paused. 'So now I just have to survive this week stuck at home, and after that I'll be free to go bowling with you! *Just* you though. And Josh if he wants to come. But definitely no double dates involving Sadie!'

My heart was starting to beat a little faster as I swallowed, feeling another warm flush creeping over my skin as I nodded and croaked, 'Cool.'

After school that day Lenny and another social worker came to talk to us. After they'd spoken to me and Sadie on our own and then all of us together they said they really hoped Sadie would be able to live with us until her dad got out of prison. They thought a bit more time was needed to check Sadie could keep her promise to stop leaving our house without Mum's permission. But if Sadie did that, they thought the remaining part of the assessment should be fairly straightforward.

Mum also had a talk with Sadie about Alison, saying that Alison wasn't mature enough yet to make the right choices for her, and that in time Alison would probably see that for herself. I think Mum's words probably helped a bit, even if they couldn't take away the memory of Sadie's goodbye phone call when Alison had ended up crying and shouting down the phone as she boarded her bus.

For the next two days Sadie was unusually quiet – both at home and at school.

I was still chairing the debate – and despite how subdued she seemed, Sadie was still holding me to my promise to organise the last-minute change of topic. She wanted to argue her case against zoos, even if it meant getting into trouble with Mrs Smee.

Personally I was far more worried about what Dad would think than Mrs Smee. How would he view what we were planning? True to his word he had booked Friday afternoon off work and had promised to be there. Since Mum would also be present he had said he wouldn't bring Kristen, even though she had asked to come. That was doubly nice, I thought – nice that he was considering Mum's feelings, but also nice that Kristen wanted to see me in the debate.

Of course there was a limit to all this 'niceness' since at the end of the day Mum and Dad were still going to be in the same room at the same time for the first time in absolutely ages.

As I walked out of school on Wednesday afternoon I was unlucky enough to be spotted by Julia and Katy, who had borrowed Anne-Marie's magazine to check out their face shapes. Of course I knew what was going to happen next.

'Hey, I've got a great joke for you, Poppy,' Julia said. 'What has a square face and four eyes?'

'Shut up!' I hissed at them.

'Or what? Are you going to set your cousin on us again? Help! I'm really scared, aren't you, Katy?'

'I'm more scared of Poppy's face actually!' Katy said.

I was so focused on getting away from them that I almost didn't see the tall suited figure standing waiting for me outside the gates.

'DAD!' I exclaimed in delight. 'What are *you* doing here?'

'My court case this afternoon got adjourned, so I decided to pick up your new glasses from the optician,' he explained as he led me towards the side street where he'd parked. 'I just phoned your mother to let her know

I was collecting you and we had quite an interesting conversation. It seems she knew nothing about you needing new glasses. And she's none too pleased that such a task was bestowed on Kristen.'

I swallowed. I'd known Mum would object, which was why I'd been delaying telling her. 'So what did she say?'

'Apparently buying glasses is in the same league as taking you to the dentist, buying your school uniform and taking you for a haircut,' Dad parroted. 'They are all her responsibility and must not be undertaken without her express permission. She also says you are well aware of this. So –' he gave me a slight smile – 'what does The Accused have to say in her defence?'

'Mum just doesn't understand,' I said. 'I didn't have time to wait for her to faff about deciding whether to let me get a new pair or not. I needed new ones straight away.'

'Needed or wanted?' Dad asked, looking amused.

'*Needed!*' I snapped, determined not to let this turn into a joke. 'My face is *square*, Dad! I can't carry on wearing rectangular glasses!'

He let out an explosive laugh.

'It's not funny!' I protested and then, to my complete

surprise, I burst into tears.

'Poppy, what's wrong?' He immediately stopped laughing.

'Nothing.' I was fighting hard to stop the tears because I'm honestly not the type of person to cry for no reason – or for some really pathetic reason like finding out I've got a square face.

'Did something happen at school?' He was sounding a bit protective, which was nice.

'No,' I said, sniffing. 'Just … Dad, I found out my face shape when I did this quiz with Anne-Marie and I didn't want to believe it at first, but it *totally* explained why my glasses look so horrible on me.'

'Poppy, you can't be serious!' He was frowning now. 'There's nothing wrong with your face.'

'Dad, it's *square*!' I choked out. 'It's all bony and angular! I just hate it!'

'Poppy, don't be so ridiculous!' He was starting to sound a bit cross. We had just arrived at his car and he positioned me in front of the wing mirror, sternly ordering me to take a good look at myself. 'You've got your mother's eyes and *my* family's bone structure – minus my big nose, thank goodness! And look at those cheekbones! You have a very strong and beautiful face, Poppy, and I'm not just saying that because you're my daughter. Now stop this nonsense at once.'

I stared at my tear-stained face in the mirror. Actually I didn't think it looked all *that* square now that I was appraising it with Dad. My head as a whole definitely looked more like a sphere than a cardboard box. I sniffed. Maybe I *had* been overreacting a bit.

Dad opened the car door for me and I climbed inside, starting to feel a bit silly. He got in himself and reached across me to the glove compartment, from where he pulled out a brand new purple glasses case. I thought I saw the corners of his mouth twitch slightly as he handed it over, saying, 'One pair of oval-framed spectacles as ordered.'

I couldn't wait to try them on, and the second I did I knew by the way Dad smiled at me that they looked good. I checked myself in the mirror and liked them just as much as when I'd tried them on in the shop.

'Thanks, Dad! They're brilliant!' I blurted out. And I was so excited I leaned over and gave him a big hug. 'And thank Kristen for me too, will you? I *have* told you that I really really like her, haven't I? And that she's so much nicer than any of your other girlfriends.'

He smiled. 'I think you may have mentioned it, yes.'

I paused for several moments, thinking about how to put the question I wanted to ask. 'Is she … do you think she could be … ?' I trailed off, too nervous about his reaction to ask it straight out. 'Dad … how do you know when you meet "the one"? I mean … Mum wasn't … but maybe you *thought* she was when you first met her? *Did* you think she was, Dad?'

Dad is usually very good at hiding what he's thinking – his poker face, Mum calls it. Today he seemed to be turning several thoughts over in his head, until finally he said, 'Your mother was like a breath of fresh air to me when we first met, Poppy. She was so young and pretty and sweet and the least cynical person I'd ever met. And yes – I suppose I thought she was "the one".'

'She told me she loved *you* with all her heart,' I said.

Dad just nodded, avoiding my gaze, and I suspected he already knew that.

'Dad, why did you and Mum split up?' I said softly. It was the first time I'd ever felt brave enough to ask him.

He waited a few more moments before answering. 'Sometimes a relationship that isn't working can't be mended.'

'But did you even *try*?' It sounded like I was accusing him – maybe I was.

His whole face seemed to freeze. 'Did your mother tell you I didn't try?'

I bit my lip. What should I say? My heart started to race and I could hear my own pulse beating in my ears. I couldn't look at him as I whispered, 'Mum told me she wanted to try marriage counselling but you didn't want to …'

There was a horrible, tense silence. I was so nervous I felt all trembly inside. If he got angry and rejected me because he thought I was siding with Mum I wasn't sure I could stand it.

'Poppy, look at me, please.' Both his tone of voice and the expression on his face were deadly serious.

I gulped. Perhaps I had gone too far? 'Dad, I'm sorry. I didn't mean –' I began, but he stopped me.

'Poppy, don't apologise. You have every right to ask questions of the adults in your life – especially me. In fact, I sometimes think you don't do that enough.' He paused, then continued, sounding like he was trying hard to explain something to me in a way I'd understand. 'Poppy, I admit I stuck my head in the sand when things first started to go wrong between your mother and me. I was busy with my career and I put all my energy into that instead of investing the time and effort I should have in our marriage.' He paused. 'Your mother and I grew further and further apart, and by the time she suggested marriage counselling, I … well, I just didn't think there was enough of our marriage left *to* save.' He sighed. 'But I did of course still love *you* – and that will never change. I'm very proud of you, Poppy. You do realise that, don't you?'

I swallowed, feeling all emotional inside. 'Yes,' I murmured.

Because I did now.

Dad smiled at me warmly. 'Good. Now … let's prepare our case for the defence, shall we?'

'Huh?'

'I presume you want to persuade your judge and jury at home that you actually *need* those glasses …'

For the first time in forever, Dad actually came inside our house to back me up as I presented my case to Mum. I wore my new glasses as I delivered the apologetic speech I'd rehearsed in the car, and I gave Mum my best pleading look as I begged her to let me keep them. 'Please, Mum … just putting them on makes me feel more confident!'

Mum sighed at that, and I knew I had won her over. She's always telling me how important confidence is, and how she wishes she'd had more of it herself growing up. Besides, she might be prepared to give Dad the icy-cold treatment to punish him, but when it comes to me she's much more forgiving and soft-hearted.

'All right, Poppy,' she said. 'But I don't want you going behind my back like that again, understand?'

I promised her that I wouldn't.

'I think they suit her rather well, don't you, Kathy?' Dad said carefully, having stayed pretty silent until now.

'Yes, Peter, they do,' Mum replied quietly.

And as they stood side by side admiring me in my new glasses I realised this was the first time in ages that I'd actually heard them agreeing about something.

Dad didn't stay long and Sadie arrived home from school just as he was leaving. Sadie gave me a thumbs up as soon as she saw my glasses. 'Cool specs, Poppy.'

As Mum and Dad talked for a few moments on the doorstep, Sadie said in a low voice, 'Well, this is progress, isn't it? Your dad actually crossing the threshold!'

I nodded happily. 'I know.'

'Maybe next time we can get her to offer him a cup of tea and a biscuit. Speaking of biscuits ...' She started towards the kitchen.

As she raided the biscuit tin and I put a piece of bread

in the toaster she said, 'You know how my social worker keeps asking me if I want her to take me to see my dad?'

'Yeah.' I turned and gave her my full attention.

'Well, I've been thinking about going.' She added in a rush, 'But do you think your mum would take me instead?'

I was a little taken aback. 'I don't really know,' I replied honestly. 'Why don't you ask her?'

'I will. It's just ... well ... she's never exactly been Dad's biggest fan, has she?'

'Well, things are a lot different now,' I pointed out. 'For starters, he's just given her what she always wanted!'

Sadie looked confused. 'What do you mean?'

I grinned. '*You*, of course!'

Chapter Twenty-Eight

Do you ever have that feeling that what you're doing isn't really happening? As if instead of actually *doing* it you feel like you're standing back and *watching* yourself do it?

Well, that's how I felt on Friday afternoon as the assembly hall began to fill up. The two debating teams were seated behind two tables on the stage and I had a chair to sit on at one side.

At lunchtime Sadie, Sean, Josh and I had met for a last run-through of how we were going to hijack the debate, and we had also told Anne-Marie (but not Katy or Julia) what we were planning.

'If you join us you won't get into any trouble. We'll take all the blame,' Sean promised her as he handed her a sheet of paper he'd prepared outlining all the positive points about keeping animals in zoos.

Anne-Marie was grinning. Like I said before, she really enjoys public speaking, and I could tell she didn't want to miss out. 'OK,' she agreed. 'I'll do it.'

So now Sadie was sitting with Josh and Katy on the AGAINST table, while Sean, Anne-Marie and Julia were sitting on the FOR table. I saw Mum come into the hall. I gave her a wave as she came to find a seat near the front.

I could see the 'against' team leaving their seats and that both teams were now huddled together talking. Josh beckoned to me urgently so I went over to join them.

'You must be kidding,' Julia was saying, having just been told the new plan.

Katy sounded equally dismissive. 'It's crazy. We're just going to get in a heap of trouble. Come on, Julia. Let's go and tell Mrs Smee what they want to do.'

'Don't you dare.' Sadie was glaring at her ferociously. 'Listen, this will be much better than a boring debate about school uniforms that nobody even cares about! We've got stuff prepared for you to use if you still want to be part of it – or you can just opt out. But you have to stay on the stage until we get started or Mrs Smee will guess something's wrong.'

'Fine … I'm opting out, then,' Katy said.

'Me too,' Julia agreed. 'You're not getting *us* into trouble over this.'

They were both angry but I didn't really care. Anyway I had promised Sadie, and I couldn't back out now.

As I returned to my seat I spotted Dad and nearly had a heart attack when I saw where he was sitting. He had sat himself down next to Mum! Thankfully she also had Josh's mum next to her for support. For a few moments I just stared at the unlikely sight, wishing I could take a photo or something to mark the occasion. Mum and Dad were actually sitting *together* to watch me!

Meanwhile Mrs Smee was making her way up on to the stage, completely oblivious to what was about to happen. The tops of her popsocks were alarmingly visible under the hem of her skirt, allowing the audience a brief glimpse of white hairy leg as she stood on stage to introduce us.

As I stood up to do my bit, I felt my legs trembling. I really couldn't do this! Why had I even thought that I could? I glanced at Sean and Anne-Marie, who were both smiling at me encouragingly, then at Josh and Sadie, who were doing the same. Sadie looked full of excitement and energy … like she was about to jump out of her seat and take off like a rocket.

I turned towards the audience, remembering what Dad had told me when he'd found out how scared I was of public speaking. Nerves are normal, he said. If you feel nervous, it means you've got lots of lovely adrenalin in your bloodstream, which is just the thing you need to get you through. *So don't get nervous about feeling nervous.*

It's a pity adrenalin doesn't seem to make your voice any louder, because I have a very quiet one that doesn't usually carry very far. But Dad says that's what micro-phones are for and today, for the first time ever, I was actually getting to use one.

'Thank you all for coming to our debate,' I heard my embarrassing, not-very-human-sounding voice blast out as all eyes in the room fixed on me. I swallowed and concentrated on remembering the words I'd been rehears-ing repeatedly in my head all day. 'And now we have a surprise for you – and also for Mrs Smee. We've decided to change our debate topic this afternoon to a subject we feel especially passionate about. So we're going to pose the question: *Is it right to keep animals in zoos?*'

As I sat down the audience applauded, and I avoided looking at Mrs Smee or any of the other teachers in the room. I knew no one would stop us now as Sean jumped up and began to present the 'for zoos' side. I felt my heartbeat gradually slowing as I listened to him. I knew I could rely on him and Anne-Marie to do a good job as they talked sensibly and intelligently about saving endangered species and educating the public and so on. Next Josh put forward a sound argument about how humans have no right to keep animals in captivity, managing to appear calm and rational and reasonable throughout.

And then it was Sadie's turn ...

That's when my mouth went bone dry and I started to feel my heart thumping again. Because if anyone was going to get carried away and say something offensive that would get us all into trouble it would be Sadie.

I'm not sure what I expected her to say, or how I expected her to say it, but she totally surprised me. 'This is a subject very close to my heart,' she began in a clear but passionate voice that seemed to capture the attention of everyone in the room straight away. 'Because in my opinion, zoos are quite simply *prisons* for animals.' She paused and looked around at all the parents' faces. 'I want you to think about it this way for a moment – if we put a *person* behind bars ... keep him captive in a confined space away from his home and his family ... if we do this to a human, then it is widely acknowledged as a severe and terrible punishment … So why do we think it's no big deal to take away the liberty of animals who have done nothing wrong?' She paused. 'Imagine being taken away from your home and your family, never knowing why, and being locked up, never to see them again.' She glanced around the room. 'I ask you, what person would *choose* that as a life? What *animal* would? Surely *any* living creature would rather its species *did* become extinct if the only alternative was for themselves and their children and their children's children to lead a miserable life in captivity with no privacy, permanently on display to crowds of people – people like us who pay their captors to come and have a fun day out observing these poor creatures' unnatural and unhappy existence … and call it a trip to the zoo …'

Sadie's speech continued over her allocated time, but I didn't stop her. When she finally finished she got a big round of applause. She sat down in her seat, looking flushed.

It took me a few moments to make myself heard in order to kick off the questions from the audience. The Q & A session passed in a blur until finally it was time for the audience to take a vote.

I wasn't all that surprised when the anti-zoo argument

won. After all it was Sadie who had given the most convincing speech. And the whole prison angle had set *me* thinking about more than just zoos.

Finally it was all over. The hall emptied and only a few parents remained. Mr Jamieson gave us a brief 'Well done' before disappearing off. Mrs Smee looked flustered as she hurried after him. Mr Anderson came to give Sean a high five and congratulate the rest of us, before whisking Sean off to some science presentation his sister was doing. Josh's mum and my mum came to gush over all of us, then Mum put her arm around Sadie and led her to the door, saying she wanted to see her artwork. Josh and his mum went with them ... which left Dad alone with me.

'So what did you think?' I asked him nervously.

'Well, let me see ...' He pretended to consider it. 'What did I think of the way you and your friends changed the debate topic to discuss something you clearly cared more about than school uniforms? What did I think of the way you spoke out so clearly, even though you were nervous?' He was smiling now. 'I think, Poppy, that I have probably never been so proud of you!' And he pulled me towards him and planted a kiss on my forehead.

And that was the best moment of all.

Chapter Twenty-Nine

After school Sean and Josh came to find me and Sadie in the art department, where we were helping Miss Hodge tidy up. The boys had just been getting told off by Mrs Smee, who assumed it had been their idea to change the debate.

'Apparently she can't imagine sweet, innocent Poppy ever doing such a thing,' Sean said, raising an eyebrow. 'She thinks we must have led her astray!'

'Oh yeah? And what about me?' Sadie asked.

'Oh well, you're a different matter. I think everyone agrees that *you* don't need leading anywhere!' Sean said.

'Well, the debate was much better than it would have been if we'd stuck to Mrs Smee's plan,' Sadie protested.

'Mr Jamieson spoke to us too,' Josh said. 'I think Mrs Smee got to him. He told us our argument *for* zoos wasn't presented nearly as strongly as the argument *against*, and he wants all four of us to research both sides of the argument more thoroughly and write an essay on the topic.'

We all moaned about that as we finished tidying up the art room together.

Later as we walked out of school Sadie said she was delighted that the audience vote had gone in her favour, and she was going to text Alison to tell her about it just as soon as she got her phone back from Mum.

'Alison will forgive me eventually,' Sadie said. 'I know she will. And it's like Aunt Kathy says – it'll be much easier for her to get by without having to look after me as well, and she's bound to realise that sooner or later.'

I just nodded, hoping she was right, because I knew how much Alison meant to Sadie.

'So is anyone up for bowling tomorrow?' Josh asked.

'I can't. Mum and I are going to visit Amy tomorrow,' I said. '*Finally* nobody has chickenpox.'

'So have you found out yet whether you can keep in touch with Amy after tomorrow?' Josh asked.

'No,' I replied, trying not to look too miserable about it. 'I don't know why they can't just tell us.'

'Maybe they're waiting to see how your visit goes before they decide,' Josh suggested.

'That's what Mum thinks as well,' I said with a sigh.

I hadn't said anything to Mum yet, but I was a lot more nervous about our day with Amy now that I suspected that any future contact with her depended on how it went. I knew there was no way I'd ever be able to relax and I just hoped I didn't do or say anything terrible.

'What about you, Sean?' said Josh.

'Still grounded until after the weekend,' Sean told him. 'Sorry.'

'I'm busy tomorrow as well,' Sadie piped up.

'Busy being grounded!' I teased.

She scowled. 'Anyway, I can't go bowling with you guys if Sean's going to be there. He's not allowed to hang out with me, remember?'

'I'm working on that,' Sean said with a grin. 'Just stay on Leo's good side at school for a bit and I bet I can get him to change his mind.'

Sadie and I walked partway home with the others, and when we were on our own, she said, 'Yesterday Linda phoned my social worker. She wants to see me.'

'Really?' This was news to me.

'Yeah. You know how your mum made me write Linda that letter of apology? Well, she got it and now she wants to talk to me about everything. Apparently she's sold that ivory chess set and given the money to that elephant sanctuary I told her about. And she's actually offered to take me with her next time she goes to visit Dad.'

'No way! So what did you say?'

'About visiting Dad? Nothing yet.'

'Well, I definitely think you should visit him with someone. Did you ask Mum, by the way?'

'Yes. She says she'll take me if I don't want to go with my social worker or Linda.'

As we passed the park I remembered I still hadn't switched on my phone. When I did I immediately found a text from Mum. There was a photo attached and I quickly tapped on it to enlarge it. The photo was of Amy in her new garden with her new big sister. They were both sitting on the bouncy spacehoppers Mum and I had given them as Amy's goodbye gift. The text said: *Lenny phoned. Amy's parents have agreed for us to keep in touch. They wanted us to know before our visit.*

'YES!' I exclaimed. I was so happy at that moment I could have cried. 'Amy's new family are going to let us keep in touch with her after all,' I told Sadie.

'Oh, that's *brilliant!*'

'I know.' I handed her my phone, my eyes brimming with happy tears. 'That's her – on the yellow hopper.

You'd never guess they've only been sisters for a month, would you? I mean, they look so sweet together.'

'Yeah,' Sadie agreed. 'Almost as sweet as *us*!'

And before I could escape, she had thrown her arms around me in a melodramatic sisterly hug.

Acknowledgements

I want to thank *Kiran Singh* for allowing me to interview her about being a foster-parent; *Caroline Walsh*, who will have been my agent for twenty years this year; my wonderful editor, *Rebecca McNally*, and all of her fantastic team at Bloomsbury; and last but not least, my teenage advisors, *Rosie Duthie*, *Hannah Duthie* and *Ellen Tullett*, for allowing me to interview them on anything and everything.

Read on for a sneak peek at

CHERRY BLOSSOM DREAMS

Available now

Monday was our first day back at school after the Easter break. I rolled my eyes at my brother when I came downstairs and saw him trying to scrape off a bit of breakfast from his school tie. At least the rest of his clothes – dark grey trousers, white school shirt and grey V-necked jumper with our school logo on it – still looked freshly washed and ironed though I knew they wouldn't stay that way for long. Sean looks a lot younger in his school uniform, though I know better than to tell him that.

Helensfield High has a very strict uniform policy – even Leo says that whoever wrote it was clearly a bit obsessional. The rules include wearing your tie with 'at least three double stripes visible below a small neat knot' and wearing skirts of a length 'no more than two inches above the knee'. Wearing make-up is a total no-no, though I once wore some of Mum's mascara to school to test out

Lily's theory that my eyelashes are so short that mascara only makes them look normal. (And unfortunately it turned out she was right, because nobody noticed.)

Lily, Clara and Hanna came up to talk to me the second I walked into the playground.

'Sasha, we've all been talking,' Lily began, 'and we really want you to hang out with *us* today.'

'You do?' I'm ashamed to say that I actually felt quite flattered. Right up until they started their recruitment spiel, that is.

'Yes,' Hanna said. 'Because Lily's got a point about how you shouldn't judge a book by its cover.'

'Its cover?'

'Yeah.' Lily explained hastily, 'I was telling them how you might not *look* as if you'd fit into our group, Sasha, but how all that surface stuff isn't what's important. I mean, you're pretty cool on the *inside*. That's what I keep saying.'

'Not that it wouldn't be fun to do one of those total makeover things on you,' Clara added.

'Pardon?'

'Nobody's saying you need a makeover, Sasha,' Lily said as she glared at Clara.

'Not unless you want one,' Hanna put in – which made Lily glare at her too.

Out of the corner of my eye I could see Priti waiting for me on the other side of the playground. I decided it was time to join her, but before I could, Raffy suddenly appeared beside us. 'Lily . . . Dad phoned home after you left for school. They've got to cancel their weekend away. Dad's got to work.'

'Oh no!'

'We need to tell everybody we invited to the party. If anyone turns up on Saturday night, we're dead.'

Lily, Hanna and Clara all started talking at once.

'Hi, Raffy,' I greeted him shyly as he turned to go back to his friends.

Raffy glanced briefly at me and then, to my horror, his gaze shifted down to my totally unflattering school shoes.

'They're my granny's,' I blurted out stupidly, just in case he thought they were my own choice.

'You're wearing your granny's shoes?' He was grinning, looking at me like I was a complete idiot.

'My granny's *choice*, I mean . . . not her actual shoes . . .' I was blushing furiously. 'She took me shopping and . . .' I only just stopped myself from launching into the whole sorry story where the shop assistant had told Granny that these ones provided the best support for growing feet and Granny had flatly refused to let me have any others. Honestly, what was wrong with me? I shouldn't feel like I had to justify my shoes to Lily's brother.

'Catch you later, Sasha.' Raffy gave me a big smile, almost as if he didn't think I was the dorkiest girl in the playground.

I watched him return to his friends. I felt a bit weak at the knees as he strode away from me, his blazer flung ever so casually over one shoulder. I thought he could easily be a model in a TV advert for school uniforms or something.

I left Lily and her friends to sort out their party drama and hurried over to join Priti.

'I saw you ogling Rafferty just now,' she teased, putting away the Jane Austen novel she'd been reading.

'I was not,' I protested.

'Then why have you just gone bright red?'

ALL ABOUT GWYNETH!

If you'd like to find out more about Gwyneth Rees,
check out her author page on
Facebook.com/GwynethReesAuthor
or email her on **gwyneth.rees@bloomsbury.com**.

Please make sure you that you have permission from a parent or guardian.